RELUCTANTLY MARRIED

VICTORINE E. LIESKE

Copyright © 2014 by Victorine E. Lieske.

All rights reserved. No part of this publication may be reproduced, distributed or transmitted in any form or by any means, including photocopying, recording, or other electronic or mechanical methods, without the prior written permission of the publisher, except in the case of brief quotations embodied in critical reviews and certain other noncommercial uses permitted by copyright law.

Victorine E. Lieske

PO Box 493

Scottsbluff, NE 69363

www.victorinelieske.com

Publisher's Note: This is a work of fiction. Names, characters, places, and incidents are a product of the author's imagination. Locales and public names are sometimes used for atmospheric purposes. Any resemblance to actual people, living or dead, or to businesses, companies, events, institutions, or locales is completely coincidental.

CHAPTER 1

Megan dug her fingernails into her palms and stared at her co-host, Adam, while the camera zoomed in on her. She couldn't believe what he'd said. He flashed his white teeth, waiting for her answer. What could she say to him that wouldn't get her kicked off the morning show? She swallowed the saliva gathering in her mouth and forced a smile. "I'm sorry, what did you say?"

"Come on, Megan. Don't you think it's true that single women who pour all their energy into their careers are just trying to hide the fact that they don't have what it takes to get a man?" His demeaning smile widened, and she fought the urge to smack him.

He was baiting her. Again. On live television. What a colossal jerk. She shifted in the cheap upholstered chair and crossed her legs. "Why no, Adam. That would be like saying men who pour their money into expensive cars are simply trying to hide the fact that they're not as intelligent as the women they work with. What kind of car do you drive again?"

Adam's pride and joy was his fully restored 1968 Mustang

convertible. His baby. Probably paid almost as much for it as his little dump of a house just outside of town.

Dale, the camera man, smirked and pulled back so the audience could see Adam's jaw muscles tightening. For a brief moment, Megan thought he might lose his cool, but he raised an eyebrow and put on his 'I'm too sexy for you' face. "Why Megan, I do believe you're flirting with me."

She laughed, keeping her tone light. "Only in your dreams."

Adam turned to the camera, his award-winning smile in place. "I'm afraid we're out of time. Tune in tomorrow for our guest, relationship specialist Dr. Lemon." He glanced at her. "Maybe she'll have some pointers for you, Megan."

She gritted her teeth but kept her smile in place. "I can't wait."

The 'on-air' light went out, and Dale took off his headphones. "Nice show. You really played it up this time."

Megan stood, ripped off her microphone, and stalked off set. If she stayed, she couldn't be held responsible for what might fly out of her mouth.

"Wait." Adam ran after her and grabbed her arm. "You're not mad, are you? It was Leon's idea." She had to hand it to him. He actually looked concerned.

Heat burned her cheeks, and she straightened to her full five foot six, squirming out of his grasp. "You are such a jerk. And a coward. Blaming the producer? Really?"

Leon came waltzing in, rubbing his hands together. "Great show! Our website is blowing up. You wouldn't believe the comments!"

Megan narrowed her eyes. "When I joined the show six months ago, I wasn't signing up for daily humiliation."

Leon put on his best apologetic face, which frankly was about as sincere as a dead fish. "Our audience loves you, Megan. The comment about Adam's car? Priceless!"

"It's only an on-air persona. Nothing personal." Adam flashed a grin, which made her want to punch him in the face.

She resisted the impulse to quit and walk off the set. Unfortunately, she needed the job. It wasn't much, but there was a possibility of growth. The show was getting recognition. And she hated to admit it, but the sparks between her and Adam had pushed the popularity up.

Biting back words she might regret, she stared at Leon. He looked like he'd stepped out of a cheesy 70's movie. With a large handlebar mustache and shaggy hair, it was hard to take him too seriously. She sighed. "Just tone it down, okay?"

The men nodded like bobble-headed idiots. Leon grinned. "Sure."

She suspected he'd tell her anything to deflect her anger. Without further comment, she grabbed her purse, left the set, and headed to the parking lot. Before she applied for the position of co-host on the morning show, Wake Up with Adam Warner, she'd watched several episodes. Adam had seemed like a regular guy. Why he'd become a chauvinistic pig the moment she stepped onto the set was beyond her.

That wasn't true. She knew why. Ratings. The first week on the job, he'd used the word 'mankind' and she had gotten riled up about it. She'd argued for the use of a more gender-neutral 'humankind' instead. Her mistake was clear to her now. That little fight went viral online. Leon jumped on it.

She opened the driver's side door and slid into her 1990 Honda Accord. She inserted her key and turned the ignition. The car cranked, but the engine wouldn't start. She tried twice more before giving up. Of course. She blew out a frustrated breath. Served her right. It had been her grandmother's car. She'd inherited it when her grandmother passed. Megan couldn't bear to trade it in, even though it was on its last legs. The fond memories of driving through the country on lazy Sunday afternoons and of the talks they had shared were too much to give up.

A knock on her window made her jump. Adam leaned over and peered at her through the glass. His ice blue eyes caught her off guard, and her heart sped up. He really was handsome. His chiseled cheekbones and strong jaw line would make any woman swoon. He even had dimples. Too bad he was a pig. She rolled the window down.

"Having car trouble?" His eyebrows pulled together in concern.

Megan would rather walk the five miles home than admit anything to him. "Nope. Everything's fine."

He stared at her for a moment before folding his arms across his broad chest. "Start 'er up then."

Despite the cool spring morning, heat crept up her neck. "I actually was going to sit here for a minute and read." She glanced around for something with words on it. A pamphlet lay on the passenger seat. When she was leaving the house yesterday she'd tossed it in the car and ignored it. She grabbed it and waved it at him. "This looked interesting."

He raised an eyebrow, and the corner of his mouth lifted in a half-smile. "You in need of their services?"

She stared at the pamphlet, the heat now warming her cheeks. In big bold letters, it read 'Male Pattern Baldness: We'll help you fight it.' She coughed, choked, pounded on her chest, and then regained her composure. "My dad suffered from this. Before he died."

Adam let out a chuckle, the corners of his eyes crinkling, and his insufferably cute dimples showing.

"It's not funny. This pamphlet says that it affects seventy-three percent of the male population."

His smile faded. "Just admit your car won't start and you need some help."

She exhaled in exasperation and chucked the pamphlet

back onto the seat. "All right. It won't start. But I don't need any help, I already know what the problem is."

"And what's that?"

"I need a new car."

His laugh spread over her like warm butter, making her insides melt. He opened her door. "Let's take a look." He reached down and popped her hood, then strode to the front of her car. "Now, try again."

Same thing, the car cranked but didn't start. Adam frowned. "It could be your fuel pump or maybe the spark plugs."

She sighed. "Great."

"Shouldn't be too hard to fix. I've got some errands to run, but I can stop by later with my tools." He shut the hood and rubbed his hands together.

"Wait, what? You're going to fix it for me?" Since when was he Mr. Knight-in-Shining-Armor?

He shrugged. "Won't be difficult."

She narrowed her eyes. What did he want from her? Why was he suddenly being so nice? She didn't want to owe him anything. "You don't have to."

He cocked his head at her, the slight smile on his face growing sexy. "I know." The spring breeze picked up, and the scent of his cologne filled her car. She had to admit he smelled good. His smile grew as he reached out his hand to her. "Come on. I'll give you a ride home. I promise not to bite."

She waited for the obvious "…at least not too hard," but it never came.

"Fine." After grabbing her purse and slamming the door, she crossed the parking lot toward his flashy black convertible. She couldn't imagine what he'd spent on it. Who would even own a car like that? Men who didn't care about settling down and having a family, that's who. Men like Adam, who saw women as nothing more than conquests.

He opened her door for her, and she bristled. Yes, he definitely wanted something from her. Whatever it was, he wasn't going to get it. She plopped down in the seat and quickly shut the door.

Adam slid onto the driver's seat and started the engine. "Do you mind if we stop by my place? I need to check on a raccoon."

There it was. Some weird excuse to take her to his house. Of course, she should have known what he was trying to do. She wasn't going to fall for it. "Check on a raccoon? Really? That's the best you could come up with?" She folded her arms across her chest. "I don't want to check your raccoon, whatever that means. Couldn't you just do something nice for once, without ruining it with your sick innuendos?"

He squinted at her. "What are you talking about?"

The genuine confusion on his face gave her pause. Maybe she'd misunderstood. "What are *you* talking about?"

"I volunteer at the Nebraska Wildlife Rehab. A young raccoon was injured in an animal trap. I'm nursing it back to health." He looked at her like she'd sprouted horns.

Heat crept up her neck again. "Oh."

He lifted one eyebrow and fought back a smile. "What exactly did you think I meant?"

A full-body blush enveloped her, and she avoided his gaze. "Nothing. I mean, I don't know."

"Okay," he said, the grin taking over his face. A low chuckle came from deep in his chest. He pulled out onto the street. "It won't take long. I just need to check the bandage and make sure he's got enough water. You can wait in the car if you'd like."

Embarrassment made her squirm. Maybe she'd pegged him all wrong. Jumped to the wrong conclusions. He didn't seem to be the jerk she'd imagined him to be. He saved baby animals, for Pete's sake. How could she hate that? She swallowed and stared at her hands. "Would you mind if I came in to see him?"

He glanced at her, appraising her. "Not at all."

They rode in silence until they had to slow down for the small downtown district of Sugar Springs. The cool breeze carried the light scent of lilacs and fresh rain. Megan repressed the urge to remove her clip and let her hair down.

Ten minutes later, they pulled up to Adam's house. The small farmhouse stood nestled between two large oak trees. The white paint had seen better days, curling and peeling up from the wooden siding where the sun peeked through the shade. The front porch railing hung in disrepair. A detached garage stood a few feet from the house, but he parked in the sun. He got out of the car and ran to her side to open her door. "He's in back."

A young golden retriever bounded up to the car, barking. Adam rubbed the puppy's head, getting down on the dog's level. "Hey, buddy. Whatcha' doing over here? You shouldn't run away like that."

"Whose dog is that?"

"The neighbor's. But he keeps sneaking away and coming over here." He scratched the dog's neck while receiving puppy licks all over his face. "Yes, you're just a naughty boy, aren't you?"

Megan laughed. "You really punish him, huh? No wonder he keeps sneaking over here."

"You're right. I can't help it though."

She glanced around the stretch of land. "No dog of your own?"

He stood, sobering. "No," he said simply. Adam sent the dog back in the direction he'd come.

A stone path led them around the house to an old barn.

He opened the door and flipped on a switch. Megan was surprised to see the barn had electricity and a cement floor. It was quite clean inside. Several large empty cages lined one wall. A sink and a refrigerator took up another. Adam crouched next to a smaller cage, opened the door, and gingerly picked up a baby raccoon. A bandage covered what was left of his right front leg, barely a nub.

The animal sleepily snuggled into Adam's large chest as he examined the bandage and then refilled the water dish. Megan exhaled. "He's adorable."

Adam stepped closer. "Do you want to hold him?"

"He won't go all raccoon-crazy on me and scratch my eyeballs out, will he?"

He chuckled, a sound she was beginning to enjoy. "No. The little guy's nocturnal, this is his nap time. Plus, he's on pain killers, so he's extra lethargic."

As he came closer, Megan became aware of Adam's strong build and masculine scent. Maybe it was the fact that he had a cute baby animal in his arms, or that he was going to fix her car this afternoon, but her heart sped up, and she had trouble breathing. She shook it off. This was totally unacceptable. She could not be falling for Adam Warner, her pig of a co-host.

She gently took the raccoon in her arms and stroked his fur. "I had no idea they were this soft."

Adam nodded. "We call this one Stumpy."

Megan stepped back. "No, you can't. You'll hurt his little raccoon feelings."

He let out another laugh that spread warmth through her. "You're kidding me."

She allowed a smile to show on her face. "Maybe. But I still think he's too cute for an ugly name like that. How about Champ?"

He wrinkled his nose. "That sounds like the name of a Great Dane or a Greyhound."

"You're right." She peered down at the coloring on his little face. "What about Bandit?"

"Perfect." Adam's smile was pleasant. Affectionate. Not like when they were on camera. It messed with her head.

She turned away. "How often do you take in animals?"

"It varies. Sometimes I have four or five at a time. Other times, just one."

Another minute passed while she stroked the raccoon, then she handed him back to Adam. He laid him on the blanket in the cage and fastened the door.

He stood, and she smiled up at him. "Thanks for letting me hold him." The goofy grin wouldn't leave her face. He took a step closer, and invisible electricity tingled between them. Heat seared her cheeks.

What was she doing? Flirting with him? What was wrong with her? She mentally smacked herself. This was Adam, the same guy who made little digs at her every day on air. The same obnoxious brute who insinuated she was putting her all into her work because she couldn't get a man.

She had to pull herself together. Adam was good looking, but not worth the heartache. She was sure of that. Another glance at him, and she melted inside like chocolate on a summer day.

Oh, heavens. She was falling for Adam Warner.

CHAPTER 2

Adam straightened his tie, shifting in his seat. They would be back from commercial break in less than two minutes, and introducing their guest. Leon seemed extra excited about today, sure it would be another hit. Their YouTube popularity was growing by leaps and bounds. It could get them into syndication. He and Megan might be household names by next year.

Megan flipped her hair off her shoulder. She was perfect for the show. Cute. Young. A petite blonde-haired and blue-eyed beauty. But it was her spunk that pushed the show up. Their little fights blew up on the Internet. Her comebacks were witty and funny. Leon had made it clear: keep needling Megan on-air, or your job is in the toilet.

Upsetting her had been kind of fun in the beginning. She could spar with the best of them. But lately he felt bad parroting Leon and causing her distress. He didn't like the way she looked at him after each show. Distrust filled her eyes.

Yesterday had been good. He'd fixed her car, and she

warmed up to him. They'd spent some time together. It was nice. They'd actually gotten along for once.

He studied her features. The way her nose turned up at the end was cute. And she was smiling at him.

Too bad she wouldn't be in a minute.

He swallowed the guilt. Leon knew what he was doing. The show would go somewhere. A gut instinct told him so. And in order to give the show the push it needed, he had to get Megan to react to him on-air.

"And we're live in five…four…three…" Dale made hand signals for the rest of the countdown and then the red 'on-air' light lit.

Adam flashed his smile. "Welcome back." He turned to Megan. "I'm excited to speak to our guest today. What do you say, Megan? Think she can help you out a little? Give you some dating advice?"

Megan's smile stiffened. "I'll be sure to let you know if I need it, Adam." Her lips pinched together, and with a twist of her head, she dismissed him. "Dr. Lemon, a clinical psychologist and licensed marriage and family therapist, has been working in the field for fifteen years. Her clinical work in relationship studies has national acclaim. I'm happy to introduce Dr. Shelby Lemon."

A woman stepped onto the set dressed in a beige business suit, her dark hair pulled back into a bun at the base of her skull, and thick glasses perched on her nose. She shook hands with each of them, then sat in the third chair. Adam focused on her. "I hear you've just returned from England. Tell us about your work there."

Dr. Lemon pushed her glasses up with one finger. Sitting next to her gave Adam a closer view, and he realized she looked a little young to have her credentials. Maybe she was one of those child prodigies. Graduated from college early or something.

"We've been studying physical response to visual stimuli as it pertains to non-romantic relationships."

She spoke in a nasal tone, and it made him want to hand her a tissue. He tried to ignore it. "What does that mean in layman's terms?"

"There are theories that men and women cannot have totally platonic friendships. Our studies have been quite interesting."

Megan leaned forward. "Really? What have you found?"

"Well, our work suggests that quite often, single men and women who work closely together hide feelings of attraction for each other." She smoothed her skirt and pushed up her glasses again. "Burying those feelings in some circumstances will actually make them grow stronger. That attraction can quickly become something more substantial."

There it was. His opening. Swallowing the guilt, he poked Megan in the side. He didn't mean to do it so hard, nor did he mean for her to squeal and jump. Her cheeks reddened, and her eyes shot daggers at him.

Oh, crud. He'd get it after the show. He grinned for the camera. "You want me. Admit it."

A small, tight smile formed on her face. "The only feelings I have for you are the ones that would land me in jail—after they found your body, of course."

Dale slapped a hand over his mouth and ducked his head, his shoulders shaking. Adam broke persona and laughed. He couldn't help it. She was something else. He plastered on his camera smile and raised one eyebrow. "Come on. Don't sugarcoat it. Tell me how you really feel."

Dr. Lemon cleared her throat. "I think that's an excellent idea."

Adam turned to her. He'd almost forgotten she was sitting there. "Pardon?"

"I happen to have some of my equipment here. The

theory is that we can tell the level of attraction by the physical responses. We can hook Megan up and—"

"No!" Megan's face drained of color. "I mean…we probably don't have enough time." She plastered on a weak grin.

Dr. Lemon shook her head. "It would only take a second. But Adam might be the better test subject. I've noticed he reacts to you in non-verbal ways. I'd like to analyze the data from my machine."

Megan nodded. "Good idea. Let's analyze Adam."

What was up with her? Was she afraid the audience would figure out she hated him? That was no secret.

"Well, then, it's settled. Hook me up and we'll see how I really feel about Megan." He gave the camera a sexy smile. "We already know she's got a thing for me."

Someone brought in a small hand-held device that looked like an old battery tester with a needle that swung from side to side. Several cords hung off the end, which she taped to his arm, palm, stomach, and neck. "Megan will need to leave."

He didn't know what he expected, but when Dr. Lemon turned it on, nothing happened except a slight jump in the needle.

She held up the device. "The machine will measure your heart rate, perspiration, and other physical responses. You can see on the display there's a red area for no reaction. The yellow indicates a physical attraction, and the green suggests a deeper emotional pull." Dale zoomed the camera in tight so the audience could see. "Now let's start with some test subjects."

A woman walked on the set. She appeared to be in her sixties, with silver hair and a bright leisure outfit. Dr. Lemon showed him the machine. "The needle is in the red area at this time. This indicates you do not feel attracted to Grace."

The woman left the stage, and another came into view. She looked like a model, with high heels and tight jeans, her bangle bracelets clinking together as she strutted in range of the camera.

"The needle is definitely in the yellow area now." Dr. Lemon held up the machine so the camera could focus on the display. "Adam is feeling some physical attraction."

Adam decided to play it up for the camera. He grinned. "You betcha."

The girl giggled and exited the set. Next, Megan walked out. He hadn't realized it before now, but when he looked at Megan he knew the machine would register something. His chest tightened, and his heart sped up. He *was* attracted to her.

Dr. Lemon raised an eyebrow. "Just as I suspected. Adam, you have deep feelings for Megan." She showed him the display. The needle had swung into the greenest portion. "In fact, I've never seen a reaction quite as pronounced as this."

Adam's mouth went dry. Was that accurate? Did he harbor deep feelings for Megan? He didn't know what to say, so he stared at Dr. Lemon like an idiot.

Megan's cheeks flushed. "What?"

"Adam has real feelings for you. Deeper than attraction. It's quite possible these feelings haven't been explored or even noticed by Adam." Dr. Lemon unhooked the machine, her cold fingers prying off the electrodes or whatever was stuck to him.

Megan looked about as stunned as he felt. Sure, he liked Megan, but deep feelings? He'd never thought about her that way. Was it possible?

An assistant took away the equipment while the doctor got settled on her seat again. Megan slipped into her own chair, her face unreadable.

"I recommend a small experiment. Adam, would you be willing to spend some time with Megan outside of the work environment?"

Way to put him on the spot. He shifted uncomfortably. Then he remembered his on-air persona. He flashed a grin to the camera. "I'm all in."

"Megan, would you be willing to go along with this experiment?"

Wide eyed and pale, Megan looked like she would rather get all her teeth pulled than go on a few dates with him. She cleared her throat and seemed to choose her words carefully. "I'm not sure that's a good idea."

Dr. Lemon smiled. "I understand your hesitancy." She lowered her voice. "I can see how you distrust Adam. You think he's a player, right?"

Megan's knuckles were white as she clutched the sides of her chair. She nodded, almost imperceptibly.

A player? Was she serious? He hadn't been on a date for a couple of months. She was insane. How many times had he told her he was simply acting out a part for the camera?

"Quite often, members of the male gender will try to impress a co-worker by pretending they are desired by many women. This is usually just posturing." She glanced at Adam. "Again, it's probably subconscious. He feels inadequate around you."

The set grew warm under the bright lights, and Adam adjusted his tie. Megan blushed but didn't say anything, her eyes wide and staring at Dr. Lemon.

"Adam has buried his feelings for you, and thus they've grown into something he hadn't realized."

He pushed down the urge to refute her. What did he know? He was attracted to Megan. That was for sure. Maybe he did feel something deeper for her, but because of his desire to popularize the show, he'd pushed it aside.

"How about one date?" Dr. Lemon leaned forward, and the tension in the room was almost tangible. "In a public place. You can pick the activity."

Leon emerged from the back room and stood behind Dale, waving his arms and nodding his head, obviously wanting her to say yes. Everyone else seemed to hold a collective breath.

Megan stared at Leon, indecision playing across her features. After a second, Adam started to feel annoyed. Was he that terrible? Couldn't she go on one date with him? Leon's cheeks grew red, and he waved his arms more frantically. She looked at the floor. "All right."

Dr. Lemon stood and embraced Megan. "I think we've had a breakthrough today."

Leon held up a cue card, the words 'live streaming of date online' written in black marker. Adam understood. Dale focused the camera on him. "I've just received word from the producer. We will be streaming my date with Megan live, on our website. Tune in to KLKXlive.com for more details."

It was Megan's turn to sign off, but she just sat there with her mouth slightly open, so Adam jumped in. "And we're out of time for today. Tune in on Monday, when we'll have local author and poet Penny Harris on the show."

The on-air light went out, and Leon rushed onto the set. "You blew up the Internet! A hundred thousand hits!"

Dale ripped off his headphones. "Did that just happen?"

Everyone started talking at once except for Megan, who sat on her chair, the same bewildered expression on her face.

Adam squeezed her hand. "You okay?"

She nodded. "Yeah. I guess I feel kind of blindsided."

"No kidding."

Leon tugged on his arm. "Adam. A word with you in my office." Then he gave Megan two thumbs up and spun around, exiting the set.

He jerked his head toward Leon. "I've been summoned."

Megan seemed to snap out of her daze. "Okay. See you later." She stood and unhooked her mic.

"Wait a couple minutes for me? I need to talk to you." His stomach flipped, and grade school awkwardness flooded him.

"Sure."

He followed Leon to his tiny office down the hall. A couple of two-bit awards sat on a dusty shelf behind his paper-cluttered desk. Leon shut the door behind him and rubbed his hands together. "That. Was. Perfect!" He slapped Adam on his back. "You were excellent! I'm so glad you followed my advice."

Confusion clouded his brain. "What are you talking about?"

"Didn't you get my email?"

"No." Adam frowned and folded his arms across his chest.

A tinge of pink touched Leon's cheeks. "Sorry, man. I thought you'd check it this morning. But no matter. You were awesome." He slapped him on the back again. "Just don't tell Megan, okay? I need her real reactions on film."

Adam narrowed his eyes. "Tell her what?"

"The whole thing was made up. There is no Dr. Lemon. I hired an actress. It was a setup."

CHAPTER 3

Nerves tumbled inside Megan as she waited for Adam to come down the dim hallway. What exactly happened today? One minute, he was acting like his normal pig-headed self. The next, she was thrown into some bizarre world where he had real feelings for her. If she hadn't seen it herself, she'd never have believed it.

She clenched and unclenched her fists as she paced. Adam was a womanizer. At least, that was how he'd always acted around her. Yesterday had been different. Nice. He'd dropped the attitude and acted like a gentleman.

He'd always said he was playing a part for television. She'd never believed it. But maybe she should. What their guest said made some sense. If he was insecure, he might be putting on a mask to shield himself. When Dr. Lemon announced he had deep feelings for her, his face flushed, the TV persona dropped away, and she had seen his vulnerable side. For the moment, she believed he did care for her.

Adam rounded the corner and smiled when his gaze met hers. A tingle spread through her stomach. His dimples and piercing blue eyes gave him the kind of looks envied by models and movie stars. Usually, she deflected this by reminding herself how much of a jerk he was.

Now she wasn't sure what to think.

Adam approached her. "Hey. Sorry about that. Leon wanted to…uh, talk to me." He fidgeted and wouldn't look her in the eye. What was up with him?

"I know."

Adam cringed and touched his forehead. "That's right. You were there."

Megan held in a laugh. Adam, cool and confident, was actually nervous around her. It was endearing. "What did you want to talk about?"

"Oh. Yeah." He loosened his tie. "I guess we need to set up our date. Leon wants to know where we're going so he can get things ready."

"I thought we could do something simple. Go to dinner. A normal date." The idea of going out with Adam was becoming more appealing to her, and the tingles in her stomach intensified. Who would have guessed?

He started toward the back door that led to the parking lot, and Megan fell into step beside him. "Sure." He nodded. "Sounds good."

"Do you like Italian?"

"Yes. Italian is good." He seemed to relax a little. "We can drive into Omaha. Which restaurant?"

"Why don't you decide? Just tell me what to wear."

A smile lifted his lips. "Dress nice. Leon wants it up on the website as soon as possible. How about I pick you up tomorrow? Six o'clock?"

"That works."

They exited the building, and he placed his hand on the small of her back. She liked the touch. It wasn't overly intimate, yet it reinforced the feeling that Adam cared about her.

"How's the car? Any more trouble?"

She shook her head, gratitude building in her. "No. It's been great."

His smile widened. "I'm glad."

They stood by her car, staring at each other for what seemed to be a long time before Adam broke eye contact. "Okay. Well, I guess I'll see you tomorrow."

Her cheeks grew hot as he walked away, and she realized she was admiring his physique from behind. She hopped in her car, not sure what she was feeling. Was she excited to go out with Adam? She needed to get a grip.

∽

Adam pocketed his keys and pressed the button to ring Megan's apartment, Dale trailing behind him with his camera on his shoulder. Yeah, this wasn't going to be awkward at all. He rolled his eyes. Megan buzzed him through. As he jaunted up the apartment steps, Leon's words echoed through his head. *Be a perfect gentleman. You need to woo Megan. If she suspects anything, it will ruin the show. You must act like you're enjoying the date.*

Why did Leon assume he wouldn't enjoy going out with Megan? He liked her. Sure, maybe she was a bit uptight, but she was usually nice to be around. And not too shabby to look at, either.

He came to apartment 3B and knocked on the door. Megan let him in and motioned to the couch. "I'll be just a second. Have a seat." Her eyes flicked to Dale, and she flashed the camera a nervous smile.

She wore a little black dress that hugged her figure, her blonde hair falling softly to her shoulders. He tried not to ogle her. She walked barefoot into the other room. The apartment was tastefully decorated in a post-modern style. An oblong wood and glass coffee table sat in front of a suede couch that looked like it had been built from large, brown pebbles. Not a speck of dust could be seen anywhere, and nothing was out of place. A definite neat freak.

When Megan came back, she was wearing black heels that made her legs look fantastic. "Okay. I'm ready."

"Nice place. I love the furniture."

A smile lit up her face. "Thanks. I saved for months to buy this set." She looked around and frowned. "My mother hates it."

Why would her mother tell her that? It really bothered Megan by the look on her face.

"She must not have good taste."

Megan didn't seem to hear him for a second, frowning and staring at her furniture. Then she looked up and smiled. "You're probably right. Let's go."

The drive to Omaha was comfortable, although quiet. Dale sat in the back filming them, even though there wasn't much conversation. As a fresh-out-of-college boy, Dale worshiped the ground Leon walked on. The fuzz on his lip was probably an attempt to grow a similar mustache.

Adam didn't know what Leon's end game was, and he didn't like lying to Megan. It wasn't fair to her. But if he told her what was going on, Leon would fire him. Megan was the real star of the show. She was the reason the ratings were skyrocketing. He was disposable, which put him in an awkward position. He had to go along with Leon for now. Hopefully, the gag would be up soon.

They entered Bucatini, the smell of tomato and basil making his mouth water. A short peppy girl in her early twenties gave them leather menus and showed them to their table. It was a white tablecloth and crystal sconce type of place. Dale hovered over them with the camera, blocking the aisle. Several people glared at them.

A man in a tux with a receding hairline and a round belly

bustled up to them, his gaze nervously ping-ponging from Adam to the camera and back again. "I'm sorry, sir. We cannot allow this in our restaurant."

Adam cleared his throat and put on a diplomatic smile. "Our producer spoke to the owner. He assured us we could film here."

The man squared his shoulders and frowned. "I have heard nothing from him. I'm afraid I have to ask you to put the camera away."

Megan stood. "I'm sure we can come up with a compromise. I would hate for your lovely restaurant to miss out on this opportunity for publicity. Maybe you have a more private table?" She smiled, and the man's face softened.

"Let me see what we can do." He rushed off. Adam was impressed with the way Megan handled the situation. Diplomatic, and yet persuasive enough to get them what they wanted. A few minutes later, they were relocated to a table in another room.

After they were seated again, Megan opened her menu, and her eyes widened. He knew the place was pricey, but taking her to a burger joint would have been stupid. He wanted her to know he had more class than that.

His job at the station didn't pay a lot, but he could splurge once in a while. Actually, he'd tried to get Leon to spring for the date, but he was too much of a tightwad. "If the show gets picked up for syndication, I'll reimburse you," he'd said. Sure. Adam knew the conversation would be forgotten. No matter. He could afford one nice dinner. He motioned to the menu. "Order whatever you want."

A slight smile tugged at her lips. "Even the Strangozzi al Tarufo Nero?"

The mischievous look on her face piqued his curiosity, and he opened his menu. *Sixty dollars for one dish?* He choked, pounding a fist into his chest. Guessing from the look on Megan's face, he'd turned three shades of purple.

Megan laughed. "I'm teasing. I don't even know what half the things on this menu are. I'm tempted to order off the kids menu and get spaghetti and meatballs."

Her smile made her eyes sparkle. He'd never noticed it before. It looked good on her. "Why not? We can eat like kids. I haven't had mac and cheese in forever."

She leaned over, her teeth showing as her grin widened. "I dare you."

"You're on."

The waitress approached the table, eyeballing Dale, who was kneeling in the aisle now that they were away from everyone else. "What can I get you to drink? Our featured wine this evening is a lovely sauvignon blanc."

A devilish look flashed across Megan's face before she looked up at the waitress. "Do you have any apple juice?"

Adam hid a smile.

The waitress curled a piece of her dark hair behind her ear. "We have some excellent sparkling juice."

Megan shook her head. "No, I mean like the kind that comes in a little box. With a straw."

A small laugh tried to escape, but Adam covered it up with a cough. The waitress's eyebrows raised, and she looked between the two of them, then over at Dale. Her lips formed a tight line, like she didn't want to be the brunt of any YouTube prank. "Sure. We can get you a juice box. And what about you, sir?" She turned her attention to Adam.

Not to be out done by Megan, he cleared his throat. "Do you have any chocolate milk?" He tossed her his best on-air smile.

The waitress narrowed her eyes, then stepped back as recognition filled her face. "You're Adam Warner, from the morning show!" She smiled, much warmer this time, changing her angle to be in the shot. "I'm sure we can come up with some for you, Mr. Warner."

"Thank you."

"I'll give you a few minutes to look over your menu."

Megan looked up. "Oh, I already know what I want."

The waitress appeared overly happy to take their order. "All right. Go ahead."

"I would like the spaghetti and meatball kid's meal."

Unfazed, she scribbled on her notepad and turned to Adam. "And you?"

"Macaroni and cheese."

"Of course." She made a note, then took their menus. "We'll have that right out for you." She left with swaying hips.

He leaned closer to Megan, glad to have some time alone with her. Well, as alone as it gets, considering Dale was filming them. "Tell me something about yourself that I don't know."

A thoughtful look came over her. "I graduated from Colorado State University."

"Nope. Already knew that."

She frowned. "I worked in radio for two years before moving here."

He shook his head. "Already knew that, too."

"How'd you know that? You checking up on me?"

A small shrug lifted his shoulders. "Leon and I went over the applicants together before you were hired."

"Ah, I see." She brushed a blonde strand of hair from her face. "How about this: when I was seven, I decided I was going to start up my own cleaning business. I typed up my rates on a piece of paper and went around the neighborhood selling my services."

A smile tugged at his lips. "What kinds of services?"

"Dusting was a dollar, vacuuming was three dollars, and flushing the toilet was five cents."

He held in a laugh. "Wow. Five cents for a flush, huh? Did anyone take you up on it?"

"Old Mrs. Fielding asked me in, and she bought all three services. Then she gave me cookies and milk, and a grocery bag full of canned vegetables to take home, along with a generous tip." Megan's smile faded. "Mom was furious when she got home from work. Said three neighbors called her and asked if we were okay. She was mortified that I'd embarrassed her like that."

"Aw, you were just being a kid. I think it was quite entrepreneurial of you."

She stared off into the distance, a slight frown on her face. He was about to ask her more about it, but the waitress returned with their drinks. "Here you go." She set the juice box in front of Megan and grinned. "Your chocolate milk, Mr. Warner." She practically glowed as she set his glass down. "The food will be ready shortly."

"Thank you." Megan called after the waitress, then shifted in her seat to look at Adam. "You have family nearby?"

"Yes. My father lives in Iowa."

"My cousin lives in Iowa. Where's your dad at?" She picked up her juice box and pulled the straw off the back.

He waved his hand, fully aware that the camera was rolling. "A small enough town I'm sure you've never heard of it."

She raised an eyebrow but didn't push it, and he inwardly sighed with relief. That was a conversation he didn't want to have in front of the cameras. In fact, he was hoping he wouldn't have to have it at all. His father was the last thing he wanted to discuss.

CHAPTER 4

Their meals arrived, and Megan marveled as Adam fumbled with his silverware. Why was he so nervous? She contemplated the possibility, as she had over the past couple of days, that he might have secret feelings for her.

Of course, the idea of Adam quietly pining away for her was flattering. Any girl would think so. Being wanted by a man was a special kind of thrill. But Adam? With his broad shoulders and gorgeous eyes, it was like she was back in high school and the captain of the football team had asked her to prom.

Adam pointed to her plate. "How's your spaghetti?"

"I think I've died and gone to heaven." She twirled a long piece around her fork. "I don't know what they did, but this is the best sauce I've ever tasted. And I think this pasta is freshly made."

"I agree. This macaroni is delicious. Kids eat like kings here."

The way he was looking at her—intently, with one eyebrow slightly raised—made her insides tingle. She could have sworn he'd grown more handsome in the last few minutes.

His gaze grew intense, and she squirmed. "Your turn to tell me something I don't know."

"When I bought my Mustang, it was a heap of junk. Got it for a song. I've spent the last four years restoring it."

"I knew you were good with cars, but I had no idea you could restore them. Your car is beautiful."

"Thanks. The paint job wasn't cheap, but it was worth it."

Megan popped a meatball into her mouth, savoring the flavor. After she swallowed, she said, "So, you restore cars and save baby animals. What else don't I know about you?"

He thought for a moment. "I'm a terrible dancer."

Megan laughed. "Really?"

"Horrible. As in, my homecoming date dumped me for Fred Dunn. In the middle of the dance. I guess she got tired of me embarrassing her."

"Aw, that's sad." She tried not to giggle, but failed.

"And I can't carry a tune. Don't make me sing, it's not pretty." He grinned, then took a swig of his chocolate milk.

"I guess if we're confessing things we stink at, I'll admit I can't draw. Not even stick figures. In fact, it's not a good idea to get me near paint, either. Or pottery. I, uh, got kicked out of seventh grade art class."

Adam choked on his milk. "No way. How?"

"It wasn't entirely my fault. I don't think the teacher made it very clear that our clay needed to be hollowed out if we had any solid areas."

He hid a smile. "Oh, no."

"Oh, yes. Mine exploded in the kiln. Ruined a bunch of other kid's projects. And Parent's Night was the next day." She picked up her fork and stabbed a meatball. "That's when Mrs. Bohate suggested I try shop class instead."

"How did that go?"

She took another bite as Dale moved to get a better shot. She'd almost forgotten he was there. "It wasn't a good fit either. Power tools and I don't get along. Mr. Harding banned me from using the scroll saw."

The corner of his mouth lifted up in a grin. "At least you still have all your fingers."

"I think he was more worried about me breaking the machine than hurting myself."

He chuckled. "Any other little-known facts I should know about you?"

She twirled the last of her spaghetti around her fork. "I've never been on a Ferris wheel."

"Really?"

"To be honest, they scare me. I'm not good with heights."

He arched an eyebrow, which looked really sexy on him. "Any heights?"

"Just those that are off the floor."

A warm laugh erupted from his chest. "Got it."

The waitress sauntered up to the table, her hand on her hip, eyeballing the camera. "Is everything good here?"

Adam leaned forward. "Excellent. The best kid's meal I've had in years."

She tittered and put her hand on his shoulder. Megan fought the urge to slap her as the perky little waitress leaned over Adam. "You're so funny, Mr. Warner."

"Seriously? You're flirting with my date?" Megan blurted. When they both stared at her, she wished she had kept her mouth shut.

The waitress stiffened. "No. I'm doing my job." She picked up the empty plates and stalked off with a sniff.

Adam grinned. "Are you jealous of our waitress?"

A snort came out of Megan, which she tried to cover up with a cough. "Hardly."

He chuckled. "Would you like dessert?"

"I'm full, thanks." For some reason, she wasn't in the mood to sit at the table any longer. Having to watch some waitress fawn all over Adam was making her head hurt.

"How about this. I know a little place that makes old fashioned milkshakes. The kind with real whipped cream on top." The way his face lit up was endearing.

"Sounds yummy. I'm in. Let's blow this joint."

He paid the check and they piled back into Adam's car. Megan found herself relaxing and enjoying the time with him, even though they were on camera. It was getting easier to forget about being filmed as they talked.

The shake shop was a quaint little restaurant on the corner, with a red and white striped awning and a checkered tile floor. They were severely overdressed, but Megan found herself having fun anyway. The waitress wore a poodle skirt and saddle shoes, and she acted like she didn't even notice Dale. "Whaddya want tonight, hun?" she asked as she smacked her gum.

They ordered strawberry shakes with extra whipped cream. As people came in, they stared. It was hard to blend in with what they were wearing and Dale climbing all over the adjacent booth to get a good angle, but Adam just smiled conspiratorially and made it into a game.

"Act like nothing's out of the ordinary. We dress like this all the time."

She giggled. "And the paparazzi follow us around."

"We're perfectly normal." Adam grabbed his cherry by the stem and raised it in the air so he could eat it. A bit of whipped cream stuck to his upper lip. She laughed, and he shot her a quizzical grin. "What?"

"You've got something…on your…" She pointed to her own lip, and he swiped at his mouth with his napkin but didn't get it.

"Here." She reached across the table and wiped his lip

with her thumb. Electricity zinged up her arm, and she yanked her hand back. Her heart pounded in her chest.

He sat there grinning, apparently unaffected by the physical contact, while her head spun. She stared at his lips, wondering what it would be like to kiss him, then mentally smacked herself for thinking it. But she found her gaze being drawn to his mouth the rest of the evening.

~

Adam pulled into Megan's apartment complex parking lot and stopped the car. He'd had a surprisingly good time with her this evening. She'd let her guard down. Had some fun. He didn't want the date to end. "I'll walk you to your door."

He ran around and acted the gentleman, helping her out of the car. Dale trailed after them, into the building, and up the steps. It wasn't until they were standing awkwardly in front of her door that the thought occurred to him Leon might be expecting him to kiss Megan goodnight. He smiled and shoved his hands in his suit pockets. He wasn't going to do anything she wasn't comfortable with, and Leon could just deal with it.

She stared up at him. "I had a good time tonight." Her eyelashes brushed her cheeks as she glanced at the floor. "If you would have told me last week that I'd enjoy a date with you, I never would have believed it."

"And that's why the guys like you so much. You know how to boost their confidence."

She let out a little giggle. "I think it sounds a bit silly, but..." She shifted her weight and had trouble looking him in the eye. "It made a difference, what Dr. Lemon said. It made me realize I shouldn't judge people by the masks they wear."

Bringing up the fake Dr. Lemon made his mouth go dry,

and guilt formed in his gut. Why had Leon done that? And what was he supposed to say to Megan? He cleared his throat. "I don't know if I would put too much stock in that machine."

She touched his arm. "You don't have to be embarrassed. Feelings are never wrong."

What he was feeling right now was the urge to punch Leon for putting him in this situation. Best to change the subject completely. "I had a good time tonight, too."

A shy smile crept onto her face. "Maybe we can do it again sometime."

"I'd like that."

Before he knew what was happening, Megan stood on her tip toes and brushed a feather light kiss across his lips. The sensation was both sweet and thrilling, but she stepped away before he could fully process it. Instinct took over, and he wrapped his arms around her, pulling her close. He kissed her, gently at first, but when she responded to him he grew more passionate. Her lips were soft and smooth, and he wanted to drink her in. She entwined her fingers in his hair, and he pulled her even closer, the warmth of her body making him weak in the knees.

As he kissed her, the world around him melted away and all his sensations heightened. He suddenly didn't want to do anything else but hold her in his arms and taste her sweet kiss.

She pulled back, and he stared into Megan's eyes, completely lost in the pools of blue. He knew he should say something, but no words would form in his head. His pulse raced, and he couldn't seem to catch his breath. He felt like a school boy, all awkward and yet exhilarated.

Megan glanced at the camera and blushed.

He'd forgotten they were broadcasting—live—on the Internet. He took a step back. "Well, uh, goodnight."

Her blush deepened. "See you."

After she entered her apartment, he couldn't help but stare at the empty hall and wonder what had just happened.

~

Megan leaned her back against her door, her heart pounding. Kissing Adam had been everything she'd imagined and more. Electrifying would be an understatement. She wouldn't be surprised to look in the mirror and see her hair standing on end. His touch had sent tingles through her entire body. She could barely breathe.

Her phone rang, snapping her back to reality. She fished it out of her purse and looked at the display. Wendy.

"Hey little sis. What's up?"

"O-M-G girl, tell me everything."

Megan scrunched up her nose. "What?"

"Your date, stupid. I watched you kiss Adam Warner! That was no little peck on the lips. Tell all."

Her head swam. "Since when do you watch the show?"

"It's all over my Twitter feed. Your co-host is a hottie!"

If Wendy had seen it online, they must have gotten a ton of hits. Leon would be ecstatic. She sunk into her armchair. "Yeah, he's cute."

"Everyone's talking about how you fight on the show, but he's secretly in love with you. Is that true?" Her voice rose in pitch.

What could she say to that? The same question had been going through her mind all night. "I don't know."

"Wow, the website now says, 'Watch the second date, coming soon.' When is that?"

Wendy's words snapped her out of the fog that Adam's kiss had created. "What? I never agreed to a second date."

"You did say you wanted to do it again sometime."

Megan stood, clutching the phone tight. "Yeah, but I meant alone, not on camera. Leon is such a jerk! I gotta go. He must be at the station right now."

Megan hung up the phone and shoved it back into her purse. He had some nerve putting that up without even asking her. She grabbed her keys and opened her door. Who did Leon think he was, anyway, presuming to tape her budding romance for his own profit? She had better straighten him out.

She raced down to the station. Sure enough, Leon's car was parked in the lot…right beside Adam's car. What was he doing here? Maybe dropping Dale off?

The night air had gotten chilly, but she ignored the cold as she entered the station. She stomped down the hallway but slowed as she heard voices coming from Leon's office. The door was ajar, and she could see Leon, Dale, and Adam all crowded around the computer screen.

"Adam, the kiss was brilliant. We've got half-a-million hits and rising." Leon slugged him on the shoulder. "The way you kissed her, no one will ever suspect a thing."

Heat flushed through her body, and her stomach tightened. What was he talking about? She crept closer to the wall so she wouldn't be visible if one of them turned around.

Dale laughed. "*I* almost believed you had feelings for her. And I watch you two fight every day."

"Listen," Leon said. "About the fighting. You should keep things cool for a while. Flirt a little more. After the next few dates, it will come out that Dr. Lemon is a fraud and this was all a publicity stunt. Megan's going to blow her top. We'll make national news!"

Megan clenched her fists, her nails biting into her skin. This was all a lie, and Adam was in on it. She turned on her heel and ran down the hall before she could hear any more, tears blurring her vision.

How could he do this to her, make her think he cared for her, then laugh at her when she found out the truth? She was such a fool. How could she have fallen for the stupid machine-that-reads-feelings? What an idiot she was.

She shivered as she approached her car and slid into the driver's seat. Humiliation burned in her, and she ground her teeth. Maybe she was stupid, but Leon was right about one thing. They *would* make national news. But she'd make sure *she* wasn't the one they were laughing at.

CHAPTER 5

Adam reeled back in shock. "Wait, what? You can't do that to Megan."

Leon stared at him, obvious confusion on his face. "It's nothing personal. She's going to be a star. Think of the publicity."

Adam's stomach turned cold as anger surged in him. He grabbed Leon's shirt in his fist, pulling his face close and practically lifting him off the cheap office chair. "No. You're not doing that. I agreed to go out with her on-air. That's it. You're not going to humiliate her."

Leon put his hands up in the air in a lame 'I surrender' gesture. "Hey, man. Cool it. Whatever you want. I'll change the game plan."

Adam released Leon and let him slump back in the chair. "You're going to tell Megan everything. Confess about Dr. Lemon. And if she still wants to work for you, count your lucky stars."

Leon stood and smoothed his shirt. "Now, settle down. We don't have to tell Megan anything yet."

Dale piped up. "Just look at these comments. People can't

wait to see your next date. If Megan knows Dr. Lemon is a fake, she'll never go out with you again." Dale pointed to the computer, and Adam squinted at the screen.

"I don't care what people are saying. It's not fair to Megan." He took in a deep breath to steady his heart rate. Why was he so upset? He blinked. Had he really grabbed his boss like that?

"Let's not get hasty. This whole thing is bringing the ratings of the show up." Leon hitched his pants and looked Adam in the eye. "This is actually helping Megan. It's boosting her career."

Adam knew there wasn't an altruistic bone in Leon's body. This wasn't about doing anything for Megan. However, the attention the show was getting really would help Megan in the end. Wouldn't it?

And if they didn't humiliate her by spinning it as a publicity stunt, what would be the harm in continuing the dates on-air? He would like to go out with her again.

Leon frowned. "This station needs the attention. If not from you, I'll find someone else."

And there it was. A thinly veiled threat to his job. If he didn't go along with Leon, he'd be fired. He couldn't afford to lose his job right now. He sighed. "I'll go out with her again on camera. But forget about the whole publicity stunt. That doesn't happen. Got it?"

Leon nodded and raised his hands again. "No big reveal. Got it. We'll just do the dating thing. It's popular. You're getting a fan base."

Dale scrolled down the page. "Everyone loved the kiss. You've got to do more of that."

Adam nodded. That was the first suggestion he could truly agree with. He didn't mind at all the thought of kissing Megan again.

~

Megan spent Sunday plotting her revenge and measuring the apartment complex courtyard to see how many bodies would fit. After stewing over the situation all morning, she donned her running shoes and took to the streets. She needed a good workout to clear her mind.

She sprinted down the tree-lined sidewalk, past the older neighborhood homes. Painted eggs and pastel bunny window clings announced the approach of Easter. Young buds were springing up in flowerbeds in the hopes that warm weather would stick around.

Although Sugar Springs was a small Nebraska town, it was close enough to Omaha to allow the residents to have the best of both worlds. Big city entertainment was only twenty minutes away, while the small community had barely any crime to speak of. Most residents didn't even lock their doors at night.

It was difficult to stay mad with all the luscious sights and smells of spring around her. Megan found herself contemplating what she should do about the situation she'd been placed in. Leon had already announced a second online date. Their fans were expecting it. She shouldn't back out. She should go on that date and make sure Adam paid for what he'd done.

And then an idea hit. She knew what she would do. And she couldn't wait.

~

Megan slapped on her best cheesy smile and approached Adam and Dale chatting on set. "Good morning, boys." She flicked her hair over her shoulder and grabbed the mic sitting on her seat so she could thread the cord through her shirt.

Adam turned to her, a stupid grin on his face. "You're in a good mood."

"You have no idea," she muttered under her breath. Then she turned to him, a bright smile in place. "I'm looking forward to our next date. I've already got it planned."

Adam's eyebrows shot up. "Really? I thought you might be upset that Leon…you know…committed you to another online date without asking."

She waved her hand in a dismissive motion. "No biggie. Keep the fans happy, right? So, whadaya say, big guy? Should I pick you up tomorrow night, around seven?" She whacked him in the chest.

He gave her a weird look, but then smoothed out his features. "Uh, sure. Is it all set up with Leon?"

"I'll talk to him. We'll get it worked out." She sat down, adjusted her shirt, and tried not to sweat under the warm lights. They'd be on-air in a few minutes.

Adam sat in the chair next to her. "Where are we going?"

Her mouth curled up into a grin. "It's a surprise."

∽

Adam slid into the passenger seat of Megan's Accord in the parking lot of her apartment complex. It was a little weird, letting Megan take the reins like this, but he knew she was a strong-willed woman. It shouldn't have surprised him. Dale already sat in the backseat with his camera.

She'd said to dress casual, so he had on a pair of tan slacks and a green polo. She wore a cute top and jeans. "You look lovely."

"Thanks." She jerked the car into drive and pressed the gas. Wow. She must be in a hurry to get there.

"Any clues as to where we're going?"

"Hmm, a clue." She tapped her chin with her finger. "American Idol."

The television show? What did that mean? "We're going to a concert?"

She laughed. "Sort of," she said in a sing-songy voice.

He stared at her. Why was she acting so weird? She'd been acting strange at the station, too. He'd shrugged it off as awkwardness after their kiss, but now he wasn't so sure. They entered Omaha at breakneck speeds. "Remind me not to let you drive my car."

"Ha. Don't worry, big guy. I wouldn't dream of touching your baby."

Yes, something was definitely off. Why was she calling him that ridiculous nick name? He bit back a retort. Leon had made it perfectly clear. He was to be the gentleman. They were to lay off the fighting. He let the irritation slide off his back.

A few minutes later, Megan pulled into a parking lot. The sign 'Chuck's Bar and Grill' was lit up in bright red letters. It looked clean, and he could smell chicken wings as he got out of her car. He wasn't sure why she chose this place, but he was anxious to try their food.

He held her elbow as they neared the front door. A large poster was taped to the glass. Chuck's Karaoke Contest. $100 Prize. His heart stopped.

Megan grinned and slapped him on the shoulder. "Surprise! I entered us in the contest. Won't that be fun? It will be just like American Idol."

He wiped a bead of sweat from his brow. Was she insane? He'd told her he couldn't sing. Hadn't she remembered? Dale stood behind them, the camera rolling. Adam forced a smile. "Yeah. Fun."

If it had been just the two of them, he could have laughed it off. Embarrassing himself in front of a bar full of people was one thing. Having it broadcast live on the Internet where nothing ever goes away...that was something else. Maybe he could gracefully get out of it. Fake a cough or something.

Megan grabbed his arm and pulled him inside. The smell of barbecue and fried food filled the air, and his stomach growled. A young woman in tight jeans and a name tag saying "Angela" approached them. Megan spoke to her, and Angela gave them both numbers and led them to a table.

Adam nervously rubbed his hands together as he waited for the food. How was he going to get out of this one?

A look of concern crossed Megan's face. "Are you okay? You look nervous."

"Well, I...um." He cleared his throat. "I can't sing."

A devilish look crossed her face for an instant, but then it was gone. She waved his concern away. "No one cares. This is all just for fun."

He stared at her. She knew he couldn't sing. She'd brought him here on purpose. But why? Then a thought made his throat constrict. Had Leon told her about Dr. Lemon? Was she mad at him? Or maybe this was something she and Leon concocted together. It would be just like him to turn her against him. See how humiliated he could get on camera, just for the ratings.

Their wings arrived at the table, and he dug in. Delicious. At least he'd get a good meal out of the deal. As he ate, he thought about what he would do. If this was something she and Leon had set up, maybe he could turn the tables on them. Show them it didn't bother him. Somehow.

The contest started all too soon, and he and Megan sat and watched as amateur singers stepped up on stage and tried their best to win. It didn't make him feel any better that most of them were really good, hitting all the notes and getting applause.

Megan's number came up. She grinned at him, then jaunted up the steps to the stage. She whispered what song she wanted and waited for them to queue up the machine. As the first notes played, Adam sunk lower in his chair. He recognized the song. It was an old Weird Al song from the 80's, titled 'One More Minute.'

Megan sang the first line, and Adam was surprised at how good she was. She could sing. Really well. She wasn't afraid to belt it out, nor was she afraid to direct the lyrics toward him. She stared at him and made hand gestures so everyone knew who she was singing to. He smiled as the audience turned to look at him. And as she sang about how she'd rather eat shards of broken glass than spend one more minute with him, people started laughing and hooting.

She'd gotten him. He donned his camera smile and laughed when Dale focused in on him. Megan played up the song, singing dramatically when the part came about how she'd rather rip her heart out and stomp on it until she died than spend any more time with him.

When she finished, the audience went wild, cat calling and giving her a standing ovation. Megan grinned and bowed, and hammed it up. She was cute, standing up there and blushing, even though she'd been trying to embarrass him.

His number was next, and the audience hooted as he stepped up on stage. He took the microphone from Megan, then grabbed her arm so she couldn't leave. "For those of you who don't know, this is my morning show co-host, Megan Holloway. Let's give her another hand, shall we?"

The applause was deafening. As the noise died down, he

said, "She's doing her best to embarrass me tonight." More hooting. "I think she did a great job, don't you?"

Megan's face flushed, and she tried to pull away, but he gripped tighter. "You see, she found out on our last date that I can't sing. And so, to be wickedly devious, and probably to boost ratings..." Her blush deepened. "She entered me into this contest."

The room quieted down, and he let her go. She staggered away from him, flashed a quick smile, then held her arms up like Vanna White. "Take it away, Adam!" She hopped off the stage.

He walked over to the guy queuing up the songs and asked if they had Wicked Game, by Chris Isaak. As the first eerie notes played, he took his place in center stage. Instead of singing, which he knew he would do badly, he spoke the lyrics, his voice low and sultry, the microphone close to his lips.

The effect of the haunting music and the powerful lyrics captivated the room. Everyone sat in silence as he spoke the words to Megan and told her what a wicked thing she'd done, to make him feel this way about her. As the lyrics unfolded, he confessed how he desired her but feared she would break his heart. As the last of the music faded, he bowed. The room erupted in thunderous applause.

He jumped off the stage, microphone still in hand, and walked over to Megan, pulling her up from her chair. "I do think you'll break my heart," he said into the microphone. "But I can't help myself." He tossed the mic, which landed on the table with a loud thunk, and kissed her. The room exploded in another standing ovation.

CHAPTER 6

Megan staggered back staring at Adam, unable to hear a thing above the uproar in the bar. He stared at her, a sexy smile on his face, those dimples making her legs feel all wobbly. Her heart pounded from the kiss and from the way Adam had performed on stage. He'd reminded her of a panther, slinking toward her. A predator.

She shook her head, trying to clear it. Adam could melt her heart with his kiss, but that didn't mean he cared for her. He was playing a game, and he knew how to play it well. His performance, on and off the stage, would surely gain more viewers. And that was what this was all about.

Steeling herself against the effects of his kiss, she picked up the mic. "Ladies and gentlemen, give it up for Adam Warner."

After the applause died down and everyone took their seats, they started up the contest again. Megan did her best to ignore the warmth of Adam's leg so close to hers. She smiled when he shot her inquisitive glances, and batted her eyes when the camera zoomed in. If he was going to play the part, so was she.

Neither of them ended up winning the $100, although they pulled Adam on stage and gave him a certificate for being the most memorable. As they left, he slid his arm around her waist. He leaned over and whispered in her ear. "What did I do to deserve that?"

Megan glanced at Dale, then squirmed out of Adam's grasp and slapped him on his cheek. "I'm not that kind of girl." She glared at him.

His cheeks turned red, and he glanced from her to the camera, his eyes wide. "I didn't...I...you misunderstood me."

A tiny part of her felt bad for him. But only for a microsecond. He and Leon were planning on humiliating her. Adam was no friend, and she needed to keep that in the forefront of her mind.

"Now, Adam." She put her hands on her hips and scolded him like a child. "No one can misunderstand *that*."

The shade of red on his face deepened. He stared at her, his mouth slightly open. Then he plastered on his fake camera-smile, threw out his arms, and chuckled. "Well, you can't blame a guy for trying."

She figured he'd slip into his male chauvinistic role. Jerk. She folded her arms across her chest and started across the parking lot. He fell into step beside her, and as they neared her car, he slapped her behind, hard.

~

Adam tightened his seatbelt as Megan drove like a crazy woman through the streets of Omaha. In fact, 'crazy woman' seemed to be the theme of the night. What had gotten into her? It had to be Leon. That was the only thing he could come up with. Leon had said something to make her mad.

He thought maybe she would confide in him. He hoped,

anyway. But obviously she wasn't going to be reasonable. Hopefully, this would be over soon. She had slapped him. If he kept up his act, she'd tell him off. They'd be done dating.

Breaking up on-air wasn't a bad idea. It would force Leon to give up the charade. And it wouldn't be that hard. She was already pretty mad at him.

Megan sighed and put her hand on his knee. "Hey, I'm sorry I slapped you. I shouldn't have taken your comment so seriously. You were only joking around." She flashed a cheesy smile.

So much for breaking up. Leon probably would have fired him anyway. Maybe it was better to go out a few more times and then convince Leon to give up the gig.

"No worries." He slipped his arm around her shoulder. She bristled but didn't shrink away.

As they approached her apartment complex, indecision swirled around in his head. What was he supposed to do? Kiss her goodnight? Brush her off? It was such a crazy night, he had no clue.

After a few moments, they stood in front of her door, staring at each other. He waited to see what she would do. A smile crept onto her face. "I had fun tonight."

"I bet you did," he said under his breath. Then loud enough for the camera, "I think you're going to enjoy our next date."

She raised an eyebrow.

"I mean, a little stretching is good, right?"

She took a step back from him, and instinct kicked in. He moved closer. "Yes. We should try to move past some of our weaknesses."

Another step back, and she hit the door jamb. Nowhere to go now. He put his hand on the wall above her and leaned down. "I've got the perfect idea for our next date."

The color drained from her face, and she swallowed. "You know, I already planned—"

He silenced her with a finger on her lips. "Oh, no. It's my turn." Lifting her chin, he leaned so close their lips were almost touching. "It's payback time," he whispered.

Without another word, he turned and left her in the hallway.

～

Adam thought he was used to quickly changing temperatures, living in Nebraska. He was wrong. The frosty greeting he got from Megan the next morning at the station about froze his buns off. But as soon as the camera started, she was all warm sunshine and flirtation. Of course, as soon as the on-air light went out, he was once again thrown into a sub-zero climate.

After their show, Megan scampered off the set before he had a chance to say a word. He sighed. A part of him felt bad for last night. The rest of him wanted to get back at her for trying to humiliate him. Twice.

He spent the remainder of the morning at home on the Internet researching. A few phone calls later, he had the perfect date set up. He dialed Megan's number. While he waited for her to answer, he took a glass out of the cupboard and filled it with water.

"Hello?" Her voice was guarded.

"Hey. I wanted to let you know I've got our date for Saturday arranged. I'll pick you up at ten."

A pause. "What are we doing?"

"Not singing." He swallowed the tepid tap water. Maybe he should have put some ice in the glass.

A longer pause. "You're a jerk."

For some reason, that made him smile. She was the one

that started it. She could take a little payback. He opened the freezer, but his ice tray was empty. "Wear something athletic," he said, his tone light.

The phone beeped in his ear. She'd hung up on him.

~

Saturday morning brought gray skies that threatened to dump torrents of rain at any minute. Definitely not a day to put the top down on his car. Adam picked up Dale and headed over to get Megan.

"What's going on here?" he asked Dale as they crept into the parking lot, a large group of women parting like the red sea before them. The parking lot was packed with cars, license plates from all over. He noticed Kansas, Missouri, Wisconsin and Iowa.

"He's here!" one of them shouted.

And with that, the sea of women crashed in upon them. He couldn't even inch forward.

He rolled his window down. "What the—"

"It's Adam!" the one right next to him screamed.

Another one leaned in. "I'm your biggest fan, Mr. Warner."

Fans? Of his? Had he entered some bizarre world where he was recognized on the streets? Dale chuckled in the back. "Wow. Looks like the website's working."

Warning bells sounded in Adam's head. How had these women known where he was going to be? "What did Leon do?" He tried not to yell but wasn't very successful.

"Hey, man. It wasn't my idea."

Adam closed his eyes and took in a deep breath before speaking. "Did Leon post Megan's address on the Internet?"

The smile faded from Dale's face. "Well, when you say it like that, it doesn't sound very good."

"Are you serious? He really did?"

Dale nodded, and Adam's mouth fell open. How could he?

The women finally moved enough to allow him to park. An urge to protect Megan surged in him. He twisted around to face Dale. "Leon's gone too far this time."

Adam stepped out of his car. Several women whipped out camera phones. "Thank you, ladies, for coming here. We are glad you watch our morning show."

"I've only watched your dating show," one of them said.

"Yeah, the dating one is what I watch too." An older woman nodded. Then a barrage of questions were thrown at him.

"Where are you taking Megan today?"

"Are you mad at her for what she did?"

"Do you love her?"

He held up his hands and put on his best camera smile. "Ladies, please. I'm late to pick up my date."

The sea of women parted. "Go get her, then!" someone shouted.

He left the surreal scene when Megan buzzed him into her apartment complex, Dale on his heels. When Megan came out, she gave him a particularly nasty glare while the camera wasn't on her face. Then she smiled. "Hey, sweetie." She stood on her tip toes and brushed a kiss across his lips.

The small act sent him reeling. He thought about pulling her close and spending more time getting to know her sweet lips, but he knew she was just playing a part for the camera. Too bad.

She wore running shoes, a T-shirt, and jeans that hugged her in all the right places. He averted his gaze and clasped her hand. "Ready to forge through the mob?"

Her head snapped up. "What?"

"You haven't noticed your parking lot?"

She shook her head. "What are they doing there?"

"I guess they found out we're taping here this morning. They're here to catch a glimpse of us."

Her eyes widened. "I didn't realize the show had gotten that popular."

He didn't want to tell her what Leon had done. "Yeah." Let her think they found them organically.

After pushing through the crowd, getting in the car, and making it out of the parking lot, Adam relaxed. "Wow, that was something."

Megan sat quiet, staring out the window.

As they neared Omaha, guilt wormed its way into Adam's chest. Suddenly, it didn't seem so imperative to get back at Megan. In fact, he wasn't sure he wanted to do it at all. Unfortunately, Leon had loved the idea so much, Adam knew he'd be in trouble if he abandoned it.

He pulled into the Skates N' More parking lot and stopped the car. Relief flooded Megan's face, which gave him even more guilt. "We're going roller skating?"

Sweat trickled down his neck. "Well…we're going in the roller-skate building."

Her smile stiffened. "What are we doing, Adam?"

Heat crept up his back. He had to tell her. "Rock climbing."

The color left her face, but she plastered on a smile. "Great. Sounds like fun. Let's go."

It crossed his mind that he could say, "Just kidding! We're going skating!" But he knew Leon would have his head. He exited the car, a cold pile of rocks sitting at the bottom of his stomach.

CHAPTER 7

Megan put on her bravest smile and slammed Adam's precious car door. She'd show him. She'd go in there and climb the dumb rock wall so that he'd look like a fool. Her heart hammered in her chest as they crossed the parking lot, the first large raindrops hitting the pavement.

They scrambled inside where it was dry. Adam paid their way into the rock climbing area. He put his arm around her, and she tossed him a tight smile.

A couple of employees helped Megan and Adam put on their harnesses and safety lines. She gripped the rope, her knuckles white, and peered up. It looked like a cave wall, except it had colored hand-holds of varying shapes and sizes stuck all over it. Her mouth went dry.

Adam leaned over. "You don't have to do this if you don't want to," he whispered.

She stared at him. His brows were knit together in concern. Was he giving her a way out, at the last minute? Like she could back out now. She'd look like a fool. She lifted her chin. "I'm good."

The employees gave them basic instructions and assured them if they slipped, they'd be caught by the safety line. They'd be at the bottom, belaying the ropes.

Her fingers trembled as she reached up to the first knot sticking out of the wall. It looked so high. Adam turned to her. "I'll stay right with you. You can do this." The low timbre of his voice soothed her, and for some reason she believed his sincerity, which surprised her.

She lifted her foot, found a decent-sized protrusion, and hoisted herself up. There. That wasn't so bad. He did the same and stopped, waiting for her.

The hand holds above her appeared small, and she searched for one that she would be comfortable latching onto. Nothing within her reach was big enough. She had to settle for a narrow yellow hold. She gripped it as best as she could, searched below for a place to put her other foot, found one, and slowly lifted herself up again.

After a few more repeats of this process, she began to feel okay. This wasn't so hard. She could do this. All she needed to do was focus. She climbed higher, keeping her chin up, feeling for footholds without looking down. The rock jutted out a bit, but she kept her belly close to the wall and held on.

Adam kept his pace with her. She was sure he could have made it to the top by now, but he stayed beside her like he'd promised. It almost warmed her heart toward him.

And then her foot slipped and one hand lost its grip. She fumbled for the rock and grabbed onto it, scraping her knuckles in the process. Looking down to try and find the foothold, she saw how high she was.

Fear shot through her like a jolt of electricity. The room spun, and her stomach lurched. She clung to the handholds and let out a little squeal. Her limbs shook, and she squeezed her eyes shut, unable to move.

"Hey, you okay?" Adam asked, his voice hushed.

She shook her head, her throat too closed to speak. Adam moved quickly, coming close, and soon his strong arm wrapped around her middle. "Don't worry. You're all right."

"No," she whispered. "I'm not. I can't move." Her breath came out in small gasps, and panic gripped her. She couldn't climb up. She couldn't climb down. And letting go terrified her. Logically, she knew she had a safety line, but swinging from the rope at this height scared her more than clinging to the rock wall the rest of her life. A tear slipped down her cheek.

"Listen. I've got you. I won't let you fall." His warm breath brushed her cheek. "I never should have brought you here. It was stupid."

His voice was so quiet she knew the camera couldn't possibly pick it up. So why was he playing nice all of a sudden? What was his end game? "You think?"

"Yeah. I'm sorry."

She forced herself to pry her eyelids open and look at him. His ice-blue eyes held concern. He sounded sincere. She wasn't sure what to make of it. He wasn't exactly Mr. Truthful. She sighed. "Well, now what?"

He kissed her forehead, and warmth spread through her traitorous body. "We go down."

Her muscles ached from clenching the rocks so tightly. "I don't think I can let go."

"Hey," one of the instructors shouted. "You guys okay up there?"

"We're fine." Adam stared into her eyes, and lowered his voice. "You want to hang onto me?"

The tips of her toes were numb, and her muscles trembled. Could she let go and hang onto Adam? She wasn't sure she could do it. "I don't know."

He came closer, his strong chest pressing against her shoulder. "There's no rush. We have time."

Sure. Stay up here with Dale filming her stuck on the stupid rock wall while ten-year-olds passed her up. Not a good plan. She gritted her teeth. "Okay. I'll hang onto you."

"Good. Whenever you're ready. I'm not going anywhere."

She took a couple of deep breaths, then quickly wrapped her arm around his neck. Tight.

"Okay," he choked. "Now your other arm."

With every ounce of courage she had, she let go and grabbed hold of him, knocking them both off the wall. She wrapped her legs around his middle and squealed as they swung from the safety lines.

"We're ready to come down," Adam called.

They were lowered slowly to the floor, Megan's heart pounding hard in her chest and Adam rubbing her back, telling her softly they were almost there.

When they hit solid ground, relief flooded through her and she could breathe again. She jumped off him, heat creeping up her neck. "Sorry."

He took in a gasp of air. "No problem." Then he pointed up at the wall. "For someone who's afraid of heights, you sure did a great job. Look how high you got."

Her throat closed as she peered up to where she'd been.

He put his arm around her and leaned in close. "Proud of you," he whispered.

Her heart fell into the pit of her stomach. Why was he being so nice? His kind words hurt more than ever, knowing his plan to humiliate her in order to further his career. She turned away, unable to bear it any longer. "Thanks."

~

Adam beat himself over the head once again as he watched Megan turn away from him, pain evident in her eyes. Why had he brought her here? A fear of heights is very different than a little embarrassment on a karaoke stage. He closed his eyes and couldn't get the image of Megan's terrified face out of his head.

Of all the stupid things he could have done. He laid his hand on her shoulder. "Let's go do something else."

A tight smile formed on her lips. "What else did you have planned? Pottery class?"

"Nope. Why don't you choose?"

She glanced at the door to the rest of the complex. "We are at the roller skating rink."

He laughed. "That would be good revenge, then. I've never skated before, and I'll probably fall more times than you can count."

A devilish grin crossed her face. "I can count really high."

The tension between them eased as they entered the darkened room. Colored lights bounced off the walls, and loud pop music vibrated the floor. A snack counter with some bar stools stood against one wall. They paid for their skate rentals and sat down to put them on.

"You've really never done this before?" Her eyebrow arched.

"Never."

"Then this is going to be fun." The devilish look was back, and he swatted at her playfully.

"Don't get any ideas. I'm sure I'll embarrass myself enough without your help."

She turned to Dale. "Be sure to zoom in on him a lot."

Dale steadied the camera as he chuckled. "You bet."

When their skates were on, Megan hopped up. "Okay. Time to go out there. It's not too hard, just try to get used to the wheels on your feet."

Pushing himself up from the chair, he stood. Megan smiled at him and held out her arm. "Hang on to me."

He grabbed hold and began walking across the floor. She

was right, it wasn't bad. The carpet helped keep him upright, and he only wobbled a little.

A short wall surrounded the skating area, with a swinging door to allow access. It was early enough in the day that the place wasn't crowded. Megan held it open. He stepped on the hard wood floor ... and his foot shot out from under him. He landed on his bum, one leg bent.

"Careful." Megan leaned down to help him up. He was surprised she didn't laugh at him. "The floor is slick."

A teen with spiky red hair and black athletic shorts shoved past them. "What's the matter, Grandpa? These skates too complex for you?"

His friend, a skinny blond with acne, guffawed.

"That was rude." Megan frowned, staring after the teenagers.

Adam grabbed onto the wall and pulled himself up. "Do I look that old?"

Megan glanced around. "It's mostly kids here right now. We probably look a hundred to them."

He laughed. "Probably."

"Come on, Grandpa. Let's stop blocking the door." She took his hand and led him onto the floor. Electricity zinged through him where their skin touched.

He successfully balanced for a few steps, although he was bent over kind of funny. "I don't think I'm doing this right."

"You just need to get used to the feeling. Try pushing yourself forward with one foot, while balancing on the other."

"Ha! You're kidding, right?"

The redhead and his friend skated past. "They really shouldn't let people in here if they don't know what they're doing."

Megan shot a glare at them. "That kid's beginning to annoy me."

"Ignore him." Adam straightened as best he could, then pushed himself forward with one foot, as she suggested. He tottered a bit, but managed to stay upright. Hanging onto Megan's hand helped.

"Hey, that was good. Try again."

The next push didn't go so well, and he jerked to compensate, letting go of Megan and landing once again on his behind, his arms and legs sprawled out. Some worker zoomed over and stopped the steady flow of young kids so he could get back on his feet.

He felt like Bambi on ice. "Why did I let you talk me into this?"

Megan giggled. "Because you knew it would make me feel better."

He practiced for a while, Megan sticking with him. The redhead passed him again, and shouted, "Hey, Gramps, you're going so slow, I think you're moving backwards." His friend doubled over and chortled. Megan seethed, but Adam cautioned her once again to ignore them. He was relieved when he saw them leave the rink and go toward the snack bar.

As he grew more confident, his pushes became harder and gave him more momentum. "You're doing great," she said over the music.

He found himself enjoying the activity, not only the skating but being close to Megan. The physical contact was making him feel like a kid with his first crush.

"Want to try it on your own?" Megan squeezed his hand.

"Sure." Although he wasn't sure at all. "Don't leave me though."

She nodded, and he let go of her hand. Everything seemed okay at first. He pushed off with one foot, like he'd been doing. Then he switched legs, gaining momentum. He was able to make the turns without Megan's help, and began to feel confident. He pushed off, harder.

"Great! You're going really fast!"

He'd noticed he'd been going fast, but 'great' wasn't the sentiment running through his mind. "Um, how do I stop?"

"Just grab the wall."

Adam wasn't sure that advice was very good, but he decided to try it, so he veered off. Unfortunately, he realized too late that he was headed for the swinging door. He hit the door at full momentum. The carpet wasn't as smooth under his wheels, which left him doing a hopping, leg lifting thing trying to stay upright, his arms pin-wheeling in the air.

Inertia carried him through the chairs—where people scattered to get out of his way—right toward the redheaded kid at the snack bar, who had a full slushie in his hands. The collision happened in slow motion: bumping into the kid's back, the slushie going airborne, next flailing and grabbing at anything he could to try to gain his balance again, and lastly his fingers finding something to hold onto.

He only wished it hadn't been a pair of black athletic shorts.

Adam landed on his face, cold slushie sliding down his back, his fingers still clutching the fabric which pooled around the ankles of the redheaded kid.

CHAPTER 8

Megan pressed her lips together, trying not to smile. Adam drove down the interstate, and he didn't seem to be in the best of moods. She cleared her throat. "It sure is raining."

He nodded. "At least it washed most of the slushie out of my hair."

"You still have some in your ear."

He grimaced. "And down my shirt. My back's still sticky."

A laugh tried to bubble up, but she suppressed it with a cough. "At least the police let you go."

"I still think they should have arrested that kid." He touched the bruise under his eye and winced.

"Well," she said, desperately trying not to snort. "You did try to yank his shorts entirely off, after pantsing him."

"My finger got caught! Do you think I wanted the kid to fall on me?" He signaled and changed lanes. "He didn't have to go nuts-o on me."

"You humiliated the poor guy."

His lips twitched. "It wasn't *all* my fault."

She bit the inside of her cheek. "Yeah, he really should

have made sure his boxers weren't caught on your wheels before standing up."

Adam made a noise that sounded like a cross between clearing his throat and blowing his nose. Megan couldn't hold it in any longer, and soon they were both howling. Tears streamed down her face. She couldn't remember ever laughing so hard.

After gaining control of herself, she said, "I'm glad the cops didn't make a big deal of it. You could have been put on some sex-offender list somewhere."

"I think the officers understood. We did have film footage."

She bit her lip. "I think it's on YouTube already. Luckily, we've got a three-second delay. I'm sure the most embarrassing parts were cut."

Adam snorted, which made her laugh all over again. He shot her a grin, his dimples making him look super sexy. "That kid's going to need counseling."

"He probably needed it before today. What child makes it out of adolescence without a parent messing them up?" She meant it as a joke, but Adam grew serious.

"What do you mean?"

The windshield wipers swished as they tried to keep the rain at bay. Megan waved her hand in a dismissive manner. "You know. Parents screw up their kids more often than not."

His gaze turned contemplative. "I see."

She decided to change the subject. "So, what's your main goal in life?"

He rubbed his chin. "The same as everyone else, I guess. Build a good career. Settle down. Get married."

"Not everyone has those goals."

Lightning streaked across the sky, followed by a clap of thunder. Megan tensed. Storms made her nervous.

"You're right. But a lot of people do. I was just saying I'm not that original." He shrugged. "What about you?"

"I guess my career is my main goal. Succeeding at something I love."

"Sure." He tapped the steering wheel and looked at her sideways. "No family for you?" The turn signal flashed as he took the off ramp.

The question hung in the air for a few moments. "I don't think a woman needs a man in order to be happy."

"That's not what I said."

What was he trying to do, bait her again? She chose her words carefully. "I haven't made any family-oriented goals."

His eyebrow arched. "What if you meet Mr. Right?"

She exhaled, a little frustrated he wouldn't just drop the subject. "Are you proposing?"

A warm laugh came from his chest. "No."

"Good. Because you're not even Mr. Right Now."

His laughter made her smile. It warmed her, like wrapping up in a fuzzy blanket. It was comfortable. She joined in.

"Don't sugar coat it, babe. Tell it like it is."

She suddenly remembered Dale was filming every word from the back seat. She was getting used to him being around. He blended into the background now. And that was dangerous. She'd have to watch herself. "Sorry. I just meant this relationship is still new."

"So, you've forgiven me for the rock wall?"

"Let's not go overboard."

The rain slowed, and the sky turned a surreal blue. Adam slowed the car and turned into her parking lot. "I guess when I walk you to your door I'll have to prove how sorry I am."

Why did those words send a shiver of delight through her? He was not the nice guy he was pretending to be. She shouldn't want to kiss him. But her lips tingled in anticipation anyway.

He didn't disappoint. His kiss curled her toes and quickened her pulse. She closed her eyes and let the sensations wash over her. Soon his lips were on her jaw, her throat, and her earlobe. She placed her hands on his chest with the intent of pushing him away, but couldn't follow through.

"I need to talk to you," he whispered in her ear. "I'll be back in a few minutes." Then he pulled back and gave her a heart-stopping smile. "See you."

She entered her apartment, her skin burning where he'd left a trail of kisses. What did he mean? What was there to say? Her stomach betrayed her and fluttered like a silly teenager's.

No. She couldn't lose her head over this guy. He wasn't being real with her. He wasn't to be trusted. She untied her shoes, slipped them off, and placed them neatly in the closet. The fridge was empty, so she rummaged through her cupboards until she found a box of pasta and some vegetable soup. It was almost ready when her intercom buzzed. She let him through.

She opened the door when he knocked, and there he stood, leaning against the door jamb, looking like a rock star. Her pulse quickened. "Adam."

Really? That was all she could think to say?

"I dropped Dale off at the station. Mind if I come in? I can have a pepperoni pizza here in less than fifteen minutes."

"I was just about to eat." She pointed to her kitchen and debated with herself. Kicking him out was the smart thing to do, but she stared into his eyes too long, and her mouth moved on its own. "If you don't mind some noodles and soup, you're welcome to join me."

A sexy smile formed on his face. "My favorite."

She laughed. "You don't even know what kind of soup."

"I'm sure it's delicious." He followed her into the kitchen and pulled out a chair.

She served up two bowls and set them on the table. Then she scooped the Alfredo pasta onto plates and got out some cold sodas. When she'd seated herself, her curiosity got the better of her. "Okay, why are you here?"

He picked up his fork and pushed the food around on his plate. "I need to apologize."

That was the last thing she expected him to say. She stared at him, trying to figure out what his motives were. "For what?"

"For today...for everything."

"Way to be specific."

He blew out a breath. "I made a mistake. I tried to humiliate you. But it only made me feel terrible."

Unable to fully trust him, but curious as to what he wanted, she decided to play his game for a while. See what he was up to. "Everything worked out in the end. No harm done."

A look of relief flooded him. "I want you to know, I don't agree with everything Leon's doing."

The mention of their boss made her stiffen, and she tried hard to keep a scowl off her face. "Neither do I."

"I don't think we need to argue to get good ratings." He shoveled a forkful of pasta in his mouth.

She thought about his words. "Then how do you propose we get people interested in the show?"

His smile turned her middle into Jell-o. "Our online dating. It's skyrocketing the popularity of the morning show."

"Won't that get boring, though, after a while? Just watching us go out on dates?"

"That's why I think we need to mix it up a bit." He took a swig of his soda.

"Why do I have a bad feeling about this?" She stopped eating and waited for him to drop the other shoe.

He grinned. "Don't look so worried. I was just thinking that having our fans write in and make date suggestions might be fun."

She narrowed her eyes. "Date suggestions?" It didn't sound that bad, but a foreboding feeling settled in.

"Sure. I'll ask our viewers on Monday where we should go for our next date. It'll give them a chance to participate."

Warning flags popped up. "What if they suggest something we don't want to do?"

Steam rose and curled up from his spoonful of vegetable soup. "We can weed out the bad suggestions."

"Heights are off the table." She gave him her best 'you'll die if someone suggests bungee jumping' glare.

"Of course." He tipped his soda can up, taking another swig. Why was that so sexy on him?

She looked away. "I guess. If we have full control over what we end up doing…"

"Great!" His smile gave her goose bumps. "One last thing."

Oh, heavens. What now? "Hmm?"

"I don't think we should tell Leon yet."

"I agree with that. He'll find a way to turn it into something horrible."

"I'll sneak it into the show on Monday. Leon will love it anyway, it will draw people to the website."

They finished eating in silence, Megan trying not to notice the way Adam's shirt clung to his muscles, still damp from the rain. Or how her insides got all mushy when his lips curled into a grin. She cleared the table, hoping to give Adam the hint to leave.

When she was done, she didn't sit back down again. Instead of standing, Adam looked up at her. "Can I ask you something?"

She folded her arms. What she wanted to say was, "No.

Now take your lying butt out of here." What she really said was, "Sure."

~

*A*dam cleared his throat, leaning back in his chair. What was he doing? Maybe she didn't want to talk about it. Instead of coming out and asking, he hedged. "I didn't want to say anything while Dale was filming, but you mentioned something that made me curious."

She pulled her chair out and sat, her blue eyes staring at him. "What?"

"Did you have a bad childhood?" He didn't mean to blurt it out.

She opened her mouth, but nothing came out.

Heat crept up his neck. He'd better explain. "I mean, you said something about parents screwing up their kids, so I just figured…"

Megan sat there staring at him, her mouth still hanging open.

Great. He shouldn't have said anything. So stupid. "You don't have to tell me, if it's too personal."

She regained her composure. "No, it's okay." She stared down at her lap. "My mom and I…we never got along."

He'd already figured that out, but he didn't want to be rude, so he waited for her to continue.

"Nothing I ever did was good enough. Like when I made her breakfast in bed for Mother's day. I couldn't have been more than ten years old. I wanted to surprise her. I snuck downstairs and made scrambled eggs and toast."

"You were allowed to use the stove?"

Megan laughed, but it wasn't a happy sound. "I'd been making meals since I was little. My parents have demanding jobs, and were never around. They hired a sitter, but she mostly ignored me, lounging on the couch talking on the phone with her boyfriend. Someone had to cook, and my little sister was only a baby."

"What did your mom say when you made her breakfast?"

A scowl crossed her face. "She scolded me for waking her up on her day off, then she threw the plate across the room. I ran to my room and cried for an hour."

"How awful." His heart ached for her.

"She had a terrible temper, and nothing I did was right. My grades were never high enough. My performances never perfect enough. And when I majored in communication, well, that was a stupid waste of time, according to her."

Indignation rose in him. "What does she do?"

Megan scoffed. "She's a surgeon. Of course. She saves lives for a living."

"Sounds like she forgot the most important life. Her daughter's. Some people can never give praise, no matter how hard you work."

"She's got her perfect daughter. My little sister Wendy can do no wrong."

That threw his theory out the window. "How about your father? Did you have a good relationship with him?"

She smiled. "Yeah, we get along. He tends to be the soft middle to our Oreo cookie. If he weren't around to separate us, I think Mom and I would have killed each other a long time ago."

Adam laughed, glad the mood had lightened. He hadn't meant to get so personal with her. "I'd better be heading out."

Was that disappointment that flashed across her face? A few minutes ago, he'd have sworn she was about to toss him out.

"Okay." She stood. "I guess I'll see you at the station."

On impulse, he grabbed her hand. Warmth spread

through him. "I meant what I said earlier. I'm sorry for everything."

She looked at him funny, but he didn't explain. How could he tell her he was sorry for ever going along with Leon's stupid ideas? Sorry for the cruel things he'd said on air. Sorry he couldn't forget all about the station and do things the proper way.

If he could, he'd leave this job and take Megan with him. But that was crazy. They weren't really a couple. It was all for the camera. And he was in no position to quit his job. He just needed to get a handle on things.

He left, and spent the rest of the weekend trying to get Megan off his mind.

CHAPTER 9

Megan spent a week fretting about the viewers' requests for dates. True to his word, Adam had announced the plan on-air, surprising Leon, who actually loved the idea. And that made her even more nervous.

Thursday evening, her intercom buzzed again. She pressed the button and Adam answered. What was he doing here?

When she let him into her apartment he smiled, a folder tucked under one arm. "Hey."

She eyed the paperwork. "What's up?"

"Thought we could go over the suggestions together."

Relief flooded through her. "You're letting me pick?"

He shrugged. "We can read them together. Cross off any we don't like. We'll only keep those we both agree on. I think it would be fun to draw a suggestion out of a bowl on-air. It will give the fans something to look forward to each week."

Each week. How long was this going to go on? When would Leon humiliate her? She pushed those thoughts away and opened the door wider, motioning for him to enter.

They sat on her couch, and Adam spread out the papers

on her coffee table. "These are all the comments we've gotten this week, so there's random stuff mixed in. Just pick up a page and start reading." He pulled out a pen and a stack of note cards. "I'll write down the ones we like."

It turned out to be quite fun. They got all kinds of suggestions, from going miniature golfing to taking dance lessons. Adam even agreed to keep that one, as long as they started out with something simple.

"Ha, look at this one from Patricia in Georgia: 'Go to a restaurant and pretend you're food critics. Act like you're tweeting about the food while you eat.'"

Adam laughed, a sound which she was beginning to enjoy a little too much. "That would be fun. We're definitely putting that one in."

"How do you feel about opera?"

His nose wrinkled. "Not in love with the idea. But I guess I could sit through it with a pretty enough girl by my side."

"No, thanks." She giggled. "Just wanted to see what you'd say."

He playfully swatted at her. "Here's a good one. 'Make homemade ice cream.' We could do that."

"Now you're making me hungry."

He wiggled his eyebrows at her. "What've you got to eat?"

They ended up sprawled out on the floor with bowls of strawberry sherbet, pieces of paper covering almost every surface. Megan scooped a spoonful into her mouth, savoring the tangy taste. "I can't believe how many comments we're getting. This is all just in one week?"

Adam nodded. "Yeah, Leon's beside himself. Look what this person said." He shoved a paper under her nose.

"'Adam and Megan make such a cute couple.' Aw, that's sweet."

"Keep reading," he said, his mouth full.

"'When are they going to get serious and tie the knot?' What? We've only just started dating!"

His chuckle made her laugh. "I know. And they're not the only ones. Read this." He handed her another paper.

"'Adam should propose. I want to see the wedding online.' Are they serious? Don't they know we're not a show? We're real people?"

"We are a show, though. Some people have been watching us for months."

She tossed the paper aside. "Well, they just need to cool it."

∼

Adam fished around in the bowl, prolonging the drama of the date drawing. "And the winner is..." He pulled out a card. "Alisha from Sacramento! Her date suggestion is: 'Play Walmart Bingo. Create a bingo card for each other. Fill the squares with something you might find at Walmart. Be creative. When you see an item listed on your bingo card, cross it off. Loser buys dinner.'"

Megan smiled for the camera. "Sounds like an interesting date, Alisha. We'll be filming it tomorrow, so be sure to tune in online."

The on-air light went out, and Leon waltzed onto the set. "Great show today. And what a fun suggestion for a date." He looked down at the fishbowl filled with index cards. "When did you do that?"

The hungry look in his eye didn't go unnoticed by Adam. He hugged the fishbowl to himself protectively. "Last night. Thought it would be fun to draw one each week."

"Yeah." Leon stared at the bowl until Adam decided he was going to keep it under lock and key. The last thing he needed was to have Leon tossing in his own date suggestions.

Megan bit back an evil grin as they pulled into the Walmart parking lot. Adam frowned. "When are you going to show me my bingo card?"

"We'll exchange as soon as we're inside."

He swung his Mustang into a space, and they all piled out of the car. The warmth of his hand on the small of her back radiated through her. The doors swished open as they neared. When they entered the building, she pulled out his card and handed it to him.

His eyes grew wide. "These aren't things you find at Walmart."

She grinned. "Sure they are."

"A crying baby?"

"You can find that one without even trying."

He raised an eyebrow. "Someone wearing slippers?"

"I've seen it."

He smirked. "Okay, fine. Here's your card."

She stared at the paper, a myriad of words too long to pronounce staring back at her. "What is acetylsalicylic acid?" Then one she recognized jumped out at her. "Monosodium glutamate? That's MSG, isn't it? What did you do, give me a list of impossible to pronounce ingredients I have to go find?"

A smug smile settled on his face. "Everything on that card can be found at Walmart. You just have to find out which product has it."

She whacked his arm. "This will take me forever."

He laughed. "No longer than me trying to find..." He searched his card. "Someone sporting a mullet."

She giggled. "Okay, you're on."

"Rule number one: We must stay together." He slipped his hand around hers.

"That's not fair. You'll just pull me away from the right products." She couldn't hide her smile. Darn him. Why did he have to be so handsome? And why did she turn into a nitwit whenever he was around?

"We'll take turns leading the way." He looked at his watch. "Five minutes each. You can go first." A woman brushed past them, two small children in tow. Dale stepped back to let them through.

"Deal. And we'd better get out of the way, people are trying to get carts." She tugged him aside. "What's rule number two?" Her hand tingled where his skin touched hers.

"No googling stuff on the Internet."

She pretended to pout. "Fine. Rule three?"

"We both have to see the item before we can cross it off." He took a pencil from his shirt pocket.

"Makes sense. Any more?"

"Maybe we should set a time limit."

She peered up at him, brushing a strand of hair back over her ear. "Why?"

"Because this might take forever."

"I'm pretty competitive."

He grinned. "So am I."

"Then let's go!" She tugged him into the store, heading for the soup aisle. When her five minutes were up, she'd already crossed off three items, but none were in the same row.

"My turn," he said, a sly look on his face.

"You know, this middle one is supposed to be the free square. I have no idea what monocalcium phosphate is, or how to find it."

He glanced at his sheet. "Yeah? Well, you put 'Person in hair net' on mine."

"See? I gave you an easy one."

"Oh, I forgot they have a deli here."

They ran like idiots, hands clasped together, so he could

check off his middle square, Dale struggling to keep up with the camera. Megan couldn't help but get into the game, timing him and getting excited when she found another square to mark off. After a few more turns, she held up her card. "If I can find Glucuronolactone, I'll have a two-way bingo."

"I just need to find someone wearing pajamas."

She rolled her eyes. "That's usually pretty easy."

"Really? Do sweats count?" He pointed to a girl shuffling toward the frozen foods.

"No. Those could be workout clothes. They need to be obvious sleepwear."

"All right, I've got five minutes, I can do this." His face grew determined. "How fast can you run?"

"Faster than you."

"Oh, you are so wrong." He took off down the aisle, and she followed. When they got to the end, Megan underestimated how quickly she needed to turn. She slammed into the corner of the potato chip display. Bags of Lays Barbecue flew everywhere, and she stumbled, landing right on one. A loud popping noise sounded, and chips shot out, skittering down the tile floor.

A frumpy woman in Walmart attire rushed to her. "Hey, what are you doing?"

Adam came to her side and picked up a bag of chips. "I'm sorry, it was my fault. I'll pay for the broken merchandise." He stooped and picked up several more bags. Megan's throat grew tight. He didn't have to take responsibility. It was obviously her fault. She wasn't sure what to think about him stepping up and helping. Most of the time, people blamed her for things that went wrong.

The woman noticed Dale standing there filming and recognition dawned in her eyes. "You're Adam Warner!"

Adam gave her a sexy smile. "Yes."

She fluffed her hair, smiling at the camera. "Well, no harm done. Just be careful in the future."

His grin widened. "Cross my heart."

As they cleaned up their mess, Adam leaned over. "I wonder how many dates will end with us getting kicked out of some place?"

She giggled. "Let's not find out."

CHAPTER 10

Adam stuffed the last bag of potato chips back on the display and wiped his hands on his jeans. "Hey, look," he said, nudging her with his elbow. A young child in red footie pajamas wandered down the aisle, trailing after his mother. "Ha!"

She peered at him through her lashes. "I guess you win."

"You owe me dinner." He hooked his thumbs through his belt loops and rocked back on his heels. He'd enjoyed this date more than he expected. Megan was fun to be around.

"Where do you want to go?"

"I have an idea." He slipped his hand around hers, the warmth of her touch increasing his pulse. "Come on."

They went to the register, and he paid for the broken merchandise. Then they climbed back into the car, the sun hanging low in the sky, casting long shadows across the lot.

Megan fastened her seatbelt. "You're not going to tell me where we're headed, are you?"

"Nope."

She tossed him a mock-angry look. "Fine, just remember, I'll get you back if you choose wrong."

He threw the car into drive and backed out of the parking space. "There's such a thing as a wrong restaurant?"

"Yes."

He held in a chuckle and raised an eyebrow at her. She was something else. "Like what?"

Her lip twitched. "Chuck E. Cheese."

This time he couldn't help but laugh. "You think I'd take you to a kid's place?"

"You asked for an example."

"Okay. Got it. No climbing mazes." He glanced at her from the corner of his eye. "Anything else I should avoid?"

She crossed her shapely legs, and he averted his gaze. "Nothing too expensive. I'm on a budget."

"Deal. Anything else?"

"I don't want to sit on the floor, eat with my hands, or watch belly dancers."

"You're no fun." He changed lanes, thinking of the perfect place to take her. Five minutes later, they pulled into the Hooters parking lot.

Megan's eyes grew wide. "You're kidding."

He pulled through the lot and went out the other side, to the Mongolian Grill.

She slugged his arm. "You're mean."

He parked the car. "They do have great food. Plus, it was worth it to see your face when I pulled into a breastaurant."

"Haha, funny."

They entered the Mongolian Grill, the smell of garlic and ginger making his mouth water. The hostess walked them to their booth past large murals of gold leaf dragons and waterfalls.

After their food arrived, Megan leaned forward. "What are you doing for Easter?"

He stabbed some noodles with his fork and glanced at the camera. "Visiting my father."

"Oh. He lives in Iowa, right?"

"Yeah." This was not what he wanted to be talking about. He decided to turn the tables on her. "What're you doing?"

"Nothing special." She looked at him, and he realized too late he'd look like a jerk if he didn't invite her to come with him. They were dating. It was only natural she'd meet his father. But he couldn't. Not on camera. How could he get out of it?

He nodded. "We should get together when I get back. Color some eggs or something."

Her eyes lit up. "I haven't done that since I was a kid."

"It's a date then." He breathed a sigh of relief, successfully deflecting the conversation away from his father. Not that he didn't want Megan to meet him, that wasn't it. He wasn't ashamed of him. But it couldn't be on camera. He would not give Leon the chance to mock his father.

Luckily, the subject of family did not come up again.

~

Megan eyed Adam as he pulled off the interstate and onto the highway leading to Sugar Springs. Every time the subject of family came up, he acted weird. Changed the topic. She knew what it was like, she had family issues of her own. But her curiosity was getting the better of her. She was going to ask him—as soon as they were alone, without Dale in the car filming their every move.

Adam flipped on the radio, and a soft rock song filled the car. She raised an eyebrow. "Air Supply? This is what you listen to in your 68 Mustang?"

He just grinned and sang along to 'Even the Nights are Better,' in a falsetto voice.

"Wow, you weren't kidding when you said you couldn't sing." She laughed.

He grabbed his chest. "You wound me, milady."

A flash streaked across the road, and Adam swerved. There was the sickening thud of something hitting the car, and then screeching tires filled the air. When they were stopped on the side of the road, Adam swore under his breath and hopped out.

Megan's heart raced. What was that? They obviously hit something, and it sounded about the size of a dog. She jumped out, her throat tightening. Adam ran into the ditch and knelt.

As Megan approached, she gasped. "A deer."

Adam leaned over the animal, speaking in hushed tones. "It's just a fawn. Not yet a year old." Dale climbed into the ditch to get a good shot.

The headlights weren't pointed directly at them, but they provided enough light. A large part of the skin on the hind section of the animal had been ripped off, revealing muscle and bone. Megan drew in a breath and covered her mouth. The deer twitched in obvious pain. "Can we do something?"

Adam scooped the fawn into his arms, holding it close. He looked at its pupils, pressed his fingers into its neck, and checked it over. The deer struggled at first, kicking its legs, but after Adam stroked its fur, it settled down.

Megan worried her hands. "Can you bandage it up?"

Adam didn't answer, he just stroked the deer's neck and whispered in its ear.

Panic filled Megan. "Should we take it to your place?"

He shook his head. "No. There's not enough time. She's dying." His voice was husky.

Her heart jumped into her throat. She sat and helplessly watched as Adam caressed the deer, its head sagging, its breathing shallow. Adam continued to speak softly to the animal. Minutes stretched, but soon the animal slumped and was still.

Adam stayed kneeling on the grass, holding the deer, for what seemed like an eternity. Megan shifted her weight, unsure of what to do. "Adam?"

Her voice snapped him out of his trance. He gingerly set the deer on the ground, then stomped off to the car. He opened the trunk and came back with a shovel. He picked up the fawn and headed toward the trees. When Dale began to follow, she put her hand up. "Dale, not now." Then she left him standing in the grass.

The farther away from the car they got, the darker it was. Megan picked her way over the uneven surface, hoping she didn't catch a root and fall flat on her face. She watched Adam carefully lay the small fawn's body down. Then he attacked the ground with the shovel, his muscles bulging from beneath his blood-stained shirt, sweat forming on his forehead.

Megan wasn't sure what to do, so she watched as the hole grow bigger and deeper. When she was sure it was large enough, she stepped forward. He showed no signs of stopping.

"Adam."

He ignored her, continuing to dig, his face red with the effort.

She walked closer, careful not to get hit with the shovel. "Adam. Stop." She grabbed his arm.

He jerked his head up, staring at her like he wasn't seeing her. Neither of them moved for a breathless moment.

"It wasn't your fault," she whispered, stepping into the hole to be closer.

His shoulders slumped. "Yes, it was."

"No." She took the shovel from him and tossed it on the ground. "You tried to swerve."

"I should have been paying closer attention."

She put her arms around him, drawing him near. His cologne mixed with his masculine smell made her knees weak. "It wasn't your fault," she repeated.

He held her in a crushing embrace, and they stood in silent mourning for the life of the small deer. She was sure he could feel the pounding of her heart against his chest. After a moment, he released her, his eyes moist. "We'd better hurry. I saw a flash of lightning."

They buried the body, scooping the last of the dirt on top just as the rain started to fall. Megan ran to the car, Adam on her heels. Dale was already in the back seat.

No one spoke as Adam drove her home. When they got to her apartment doorstep, he stepped back. "Sorry. I'm a mess."

Her throat closed with emotion. She didn't care about the blood on his shirt or the dirt under his nails. She'd caught a glimpse into Adam's heart tonight. "It doesn't matter."

"I'm sure you won't want me to—"

She silenced him with her kiss. He seemed surprised at first, but then put his arms around her. Her head swam, and she pulled back.

He stared at her, as if trying to figure out what she was thinking.

"Good night," she whispered.

After shutting her door, she leaned against it, her heart fluttering. What was wrong with her? Adam wasn't to be trusted. She knew that. He was in cahoots with Leon.

But she'd seen a softer side of him tonight. Right?

Wait. She shook her head. He put on a facade every day for the cameras. It had to be fake. He had to be playing it up for the cameras. The whole thing with the deer was an act. A show for the viewers, and to fool her into liking him.

Anger built up inside her, and she tossed her shoes in the

closet. She'd almost fallen for it. Adam, the sensitive. Right. He was such a jerk.

But something about the evening bugged her. And when she slipped into her nightgown it hit her.

He hadn't once looked at his car to see if there was any damage.

CHAPTER 11

Adam drove down the wet street, Dale in the passenger seat, the camera on his lap. A chime sounded, and he took out his phone. "Leon wants us to film you and Megan dying eggs tomorrow."

Adam nodded. Of course. He'd known that would happen. "Sure. Whatever." Irritation slid over him. Didn't he get any time with Megan away from the camera? Where did his private life end, and his public life begin? He stopped the car in the station parking lot. "I hope Leon's paying you enough."

Dale slid out of the car, grinning. "Oh, yeah. By the time this is done, I'll be rich." He ran into the building.

The rain had stopped, and a fresh spring smell filled the air. Instead of pulling out of the lot, Adam picked up his phone and dialed Megan.

"Hello?"

"Hey. I wanted to talk to you without…you know… anyone listening in."

A muffled sound came through the phone, like she was holding it against her shoulder. "Yeah?"

Might as well plunge right in. "I'm sorry I didn't ask you to spend Easter with me."

"Oh, I wasn't fishing for an invitation."

"No, I'd love for you to come with me. To meet my father."

She was silent, and sudden nerves assaulted him. Was that too forward? Was he presuming too much?

Another muffled sound came through. "Um, sure. Okay."

He'd better downplay it. "I mean, it's no big deal. It's not like the big 'meet the family' thing." More silence, and he slapped his palm against his forehead. Why had he said that?

"Yeah. I wasn't thinking it was."

"Of course you weren't. It's just...well, my father...he's a little different." He inwardly groaned. Could he possibly screw this conversation up more? Way to sell the idea to her. Maybe he could throw in a promise to toss her down the stairs and pour lemon juice on her cuts.

She laughed. "I'm sure no scarier than my family."

He let out a nervous chuckle. "No, I'm sure not." Wait, had he just insulted her family? "I mean, he's harmless." Nice save. He closed his eyes and banged his head back against the headrest. "I'll pick you up in the morning. We can go eat lunch with my father, then Leon wants to film us coloring eggs."

She sighed. "Of course he does."

Finally, neutral ground. They spoke for a minute about Leon's intrusiveness and then hung up. Adam stared at the phone. He hoped tomorrow would go better than his gut was telling him it would. Why had he invited her along, anyway?

Megan's stomach twisted in a knot any Boy Scout would be proud of. Adam would arrive soon…without Dale. She'd kind of gotten used to the whole 'pretend for the camera' thing. Was this considered a real date, then?

She was going to meet his father. No pressure, right? She paced the room, butterflies assaulting her middle. She didn't like Adam. Couldn't like him. Couldn't trust him.

But when she looked into his clear blue eyes, that fact was hard for her to remember. In fact, it was hard for her to even breathe when he was around.

Her cell phone chimed, and she pulled it out. Wendy. She sighed and answered.

"When is Adam coming over to dye Easter eggs?"

Megan glanced at the clock. "In a few hours." No way was she telling her sister about meeting his father. She'd take it the wrong way.

"What's going on? Why do you sound so strange?"

Dang, her sister could always tell when she was lying. "I have to go. Something is about to burn in the oven." She cringed. Lame.

"Really? You're lying. What's really going on?"

"Nothing. I swear."

The door buzzed, and Megan jumped. "That was the timer. I really have to go. Talk to you later!" She hung up and pressed the button to let Adam in. That was close. If her sister had heard his voice, there'd have been no getting off the phone until she'd spilled everything.

When she opened her door, she about swallowed her tongue, he looked so good in a pair of jeans and a short sleeve button down shirt. And he smelled woodsy and clean. How was she going to keep her head on straight?

He fidgeted. "Before we go, I should tell you something. My father has some issues."

"Don't we all?" She waved his worry away. "We can talk about it in the car."

As soon as they were on the road, she asked, "How far are we headed?"

"Just outside of Council Bluffs."

"That's close. Do you visit often?"

He tapped the steering wheel. "As often as I can."

"And you didn't want Dale coming because…?"

The car sped up as he merged onto the interstate. "My father's in a mental institution." The words came out quietly.

Shock rang through her. That wasn't what she was expecting. She blinked, unable to think of anything to say.

He sighed. "If you don't want to go, I'll take you home. I'm sorry I didn't tell you before now, it's just that—"

"Adam. It's okay." She laid her hand on his arm, which was a bad decision. Touching his muscular forearm sent tingles through her, but she didn't want to withdraw it. "I can handle it."

A contemplative look came over him, and he studied her, silently.

Megan gave him an encouraging smile. "Tell me about your father."

"He's had a hard life."

Not wanting to interrupt, she waited for him to continue.

"My mother left when I was just a baby. He had to raise me by himself. And he had no family. No support system. We didn't have much. In fact, when things got tough, we didn't have anything."

The hum of the engine filled the silence for a moment before he spoke again, his voice low. "We lived in a homeless shelter for a while."

Adam? Homeless? She couldn't picture it. The man she knew didn't fit that image. "What happened?"

"It became obvious to the State that my father had mental illness. They took him away and put me in foster care."

"I'm so sorry."

An array of emotions flashed across his face. "It was difficult. I was never the popular kid in school. In fact, I worked hard and graduated early so I could get away from it. And as soon as I got a job and could afford it, I went out on my own."

What he was telling her couldn't be true. She'd always pictured him as the privileged child. Popular football-playing kid. The kind with a girl on each arm and scholarships to expensive schools. "What about college?"

He laughed without mirth. "I never went to college. There was never any money for it. I've had to work my way up the ladder to get where I am."

Megan stared down at her hands, ashamed at herself for jumping to conclusions about him.

"My father's a nice man. A little delusional, but harmless. Don't be afraid of him."

She nodded. "I'm looking forward to meeting him. What's his name?"

"Alexander, but everyone calls him Al."

~

Adam put his arm around Megan. This was it. Time to introduce her. His gut did a somersault. "Dad, I'd like you to meet my co-host on the morning show. Megan, this is Al."

His father grinned, gaps showing from his missing teeth. His hair had thinned quite a bit over the years and was now snowy white with a round bald spot on top, matching his round middle. He padded over to them in his slippers. "My dear." He took her hand, looking up, as he was a little shorter than she. "You are lovelier than sunlight."

Megan blushed. "Thank you, Mr. Warner."

"What's with this Mr. Warner stuff?" He turned and started back to his seat at the round cafeteria table. "You can call me God."

Megan's eyes grew wide, and she shot Adam a worried glance.

"Dad—"

"Just kidding." His smile grew. "It's my favorite joke. Gets 'em every time." He motioned to the chairs surrounding the table. "Have a seat."

Bright colored cutouts of eggs and bunnies decorated the common area. A few baskets with plastic grass and pastel bows sat on tabletops and counters. His father seemed fairly lucid today, and Adam exhaled. Maybe things would go all right. "How've you been, Dad?"

"Just fine." He rubbed the top of his head. "They treat me good here." His eyes shifted around the room. "Except for Harry."

"Yeah, I know you don't like Harry. But you're trying to get along, right?"

Al nodded, then patted Megan's hand. "And how are you, sweetie?"

She pushed a strand of hair behind her ear. "I'm doing fine."

They chatted politely for a few minutes. Other patients and family members shuffled into the room, finding seats and getting ready for lunch. The tile floor and antiseptic smell always reminded him of a hospital.

His father cocked his head to the side and studied Megan. Then he turned to Adam. "When's the wedding?"

Megan blushed and stammered. "I...uh, we...aren't getting married."

White hair bobbed as his father nodded vigorously. "Yes you are." He stared at Megan. "You're his soul mate."

Heat crept up his neck. "Dad, stop. You're embarrassing her."

"Sorry." A demure look crossed his face. "Looks like they're serving the ham now."

They ate without further incident, his father going on about how good the potatoes were, and Megan asking questions about the facility. Adam watched the two of them interact, the way Megan smiled and treated his father like a real person. She didn't talk down to him, like a child, or shout at him like he was deaf.

When it was time to leave, his father pulled Megan aside and whispered something in her ear. She blushed and gave him a hug. On the way to the car, he asked her what that was about.

"Your father seems to be stuck on the idea that we're getting married. He wanted to be sure he was invited."

Adam shook his head. "Sorry about that."

"No, don't be." She tucked another curl of blonde hair behind her ear. "Your father just wants what's best for you. I'm flattered he thinks I could make you happy."

He stopped and took her hand. "You're amazing, you know that?"

The look on her face told him she wasn't expecting that at all. In fact, she didn't look too happy he said it.

He back-tracked, and let go of her hand. "I mean, you were really good with him. You treated him like a human being. He doesn't get that a lot."

The concern left her face. "He's special. I'm glad you introduced me."

He sighed inwardly, glad he'd gotten past that blunder. "I

wish I could afford to move him closer to me. There are better facilities in Omaha. Not so sterile. They make the living quarters look much more homey. They're just too expensive."

Megan threw him a sympathetic look. "How much do they cost?"

"Some of them are $4,000 a month."

She sucked in a breath. "Wow."

He hadn't meant to bring the conversation down. In order to lighten the mood, he smiled. "You ready to go color eggs?"

CHAPTER 12

Megan awoke on Monday with her head pounding like she'd fallen asleep on a jack hammer. Her throat screamed in agony with every breath. Moaning, she crawled out of bed and grabbed her robe. This was not a good start to her day.

Maybe if she got going, she'd feel better. She didn't want to call in sick. Leon would pitch a fit. And who knew what would go on over there without her. She could only imagine.

She showered. The hot water did nothing for her chills. By the time she'd toweled off, she knew she couldn't go into work. Hot and cold flashes assaulted her as she picked up the phone.

Leon didn't sound too thrilled, but she didn't care anymore. She hung up and crawled back into bed, grateful for the warmth of the blankets. With the covers up to her chin, she slipped into blessed unconsciousness.

She awoke several times, her blistering headache making the room spin. Once, she slipped from bed to get a glass of water, only to find herself waking up on the kitchen floor, her cheek pressed to the cool tile. She must have managed to get herself back into bed, because the next time she awoke she was kicking off the comforter, and her pillow was a sweaty mess beneath her head.

Strange dreams filled her mind, one where her cell phone kept ringing, even after she answered it. No matter how many times she touched the screen, it wouldn't shut up. Finally, in desperation, she threw it on the floor and stomped on it. The tiny broken pieces still vibrated and continued to chime incessantly.

The next time she woke, the clock display read three fifteen in the afternoon, and her chest was on fire. She coughed, a deep hacking sound, which continued until she passed out again.

She had another annoying dream, only this time her door buzzer wouldn't stop. She tried to press the button on the wall, but kept missing. Finally she was successful, and the buzzing ended, replaced by loud knocking. The doorknob wouldn't turn for her. She yelled for whoever it was to go away, but the knocking continued.

Then her dream changed and Adam held her in his strong arms. He smelled clean and musky, and she buried her head in his chest.

"You're burning up." He stared down at her, concern showing in his beautiful eyes.

She reached up and touched his face. Stubble scratched at her palm, and his cool skin sent sparks through her fingertips. "You're sexy," she mumbled.

"We need to get you to a doctor."

She shook her head, which was a bad idea. The pressure cooker behind her eyes threatened to blow. "No doctor."

Then her dream changed again, and she found herself lying on her bed, a cool cloth on her forehead. Adam held a glass of water to her lips. "Here, take a sip."

The cold water washed over her blistering throat, and she moaned.

He kissed her forehead, then jerked back. "Megan, you're really sick. You need to see a doctor." He frowned.

She grew annoyed. "Stop talking about doctors. You're my dream, and you'll do what I want."

He raised an eyebrow, a slight smile tugging at his lips. "And what's that?"

She pulled the covers up and tucked them under her arms. "Be nice. The real Adam's a jerk."

He must not have liked that answer, because his frown came back.

Her vision blurred, and she blinked to try to see him more clearly. "But he's a good kisser."

She yawned, amazed that she could feel sleepy in a dream. She closed her eyes, and the world went dark. A few more times she dreamed of Adam. Once they were at a beautiful ball dressed in formal clothing. He held her close, her head against his chest. It was nice. She told him how good he smelled, and he chuckled. They talked for a while, but that part of the dream was fuzzy.

Then she fell into a long, dreamless unconsciousness. When the fog lifted, she opened her eyes and peered at the clock. Eleven-thirty. Light filtered through her curtains, so she knew it must be the next day. She'd missed work again. Oh, well. Leon would simply have to deal with it. Adam was fine hosting the show by himself anyway.

She had started to slip out of bed when she noticed a pair of cowboy boots on her floor. Fear crept up her spine. She didn't own cowboy boots. She turned and held in a scream. Adam lay asleep, sprawled out on a kitchen chair beside her bed, his head at an unnatural angle. He wore a white T-shirt and jeans.

She grabbed her blanket, covering up her filmy gown. "Adam!"

He awoke with a start, glancing wildly around the room until his gaze settled on her. "Oh. You're awake."

"What are you doing here?" she screeched.

He held up his hands. "Whoa, hey, you let me in."

"I did no such thing! Get out!" Yelling probably wasn't the best idea, because it made her cough, which sounded horrible even to her ears.

"Settle down." He stood and backed toward the door. "You're sick."

She stared at him, realization dawning. "That was you knocking on the door."

"Yes. You wouldn't answer your phone. I got worried."

"So you broke into my apartment?"

Shaking his head, he protested. "No. Like I said, you let me in. I mean, not right away. It did take you a while to get to the door, but you finally opened it. And I'm glad you did. You were not well."

She stared up at him, trying to figure him out. Was her dream real? Was he nursing her? She glanced at the nightstand. A fresh glass of ice water sat on a coaster. A wet cloth lay beside it.

Heat crept up her neck. "How long have you been here?"

He looked at his watch. "A few hours. I came back after the show this morning."

"Came back? You were here before?"

A blush touched his cheeks. "I've been here since yesterday."

"You spent the night here?" She clutched the covers tighter.

"You wouldn't let me take you to a doctor. And you had a high fever. I needed to give you some ibuprofen, and watch you, to make sure you didn't have a seizure or something.

And if you weren't better today, I was taking you in, no matter what you said."

Images from her dreams flashed in her mind, and she could no longer look him in the eye. "Um...I must have been out of it."

He rocked back on his heels. "Yeah."

A horrible feeling settled over her. She didn't want to ask, but needed to know. "What did I say?"

His lip twitched. "Plenty."

"Well, I wasn't myself. I had a fever. You can't take any of that seriously."

He folded his arms across his broad chest. "Uh, huh."

"I mean, I was delusional."

He nodded, a grin forming, those blasted dimples showing. "Oh, and your sister called."

"You answered my phone?"

He shrugged. "Wendy says, 'Get better soon.'"

Heat singed her face. Great. Wendy would probably jump to the wrong conclusions. She raked her hand through her hair, and it stuck in a tangle, reminding her that she probably resembled the bride of Frankenstein. Heaven only knew what she smelled like. "I need to shower."

"Oh, yes. Well, uh," he stammered. "I'll go in the other room." He backed up a step. "Are you hungry? Do you want me to make you some eggs or something?"

She couldn't hide a smile. He was cute when he was uncomfortable. "Sure."

She took an extra-long time in the shower, scrubbing off the buildup of sweat from her fevered state. She even shaved her legs, although she wasn't sure why. It wasn't like she was planning on wearing a dress. But the thought of Adam carrying her, her orangutan-legs sticking out from her nightgown, gave her the motivation.

Just getting clean made her feel so much better, although

she was very weak. She put on a pair of sweats and a loose-fitting top. As she dressed, thoughts of Adam bombarded her. Why did it make her feel safe, knowing that he was there taking care of her? She didn't need anyone doting on her, she was a grown woman. But she couldn't help but smile as she remembered the way he'd kissed her on the forehead.

When she left the bathroom, the smell from the kitchen made her mouth water. Adam stood at the stove, a frying pan in one hand, a spatula in the other. "Feel better?"

"Yes. Much." She sat at the table, where a glass of milk awaited her.

He scooped the eggs onto a plate and added a piece of toast, jam spread over the top. "I hope your stomach's better. You haven't eaten anything since I got here."

She picked up the glass and swallowed the cold liquid. "Mmm, nice." He handed her a fork, and she scooped up her first fluffy bite. "Heaven."

A sultry grin crossed his face. He flipped a chair around and sat straddling it, his arms across the back. "You don't know how happy I am to see you up and around, and not talking nonsense." His boots were back on.

She grimaced, and he chuckled silently. As she ate, she stole a few glances at him. She really did appreciate him coming over, helping her like he had. It wasn't something anyone else had ever done for her. Growing up, she'd fended for herself, in sickness and in health.

The food was gone in a matter of minutes, and her energy drained. He took her plate. "Go lie down. You need to rest. I'll take care of the dishes."

She protested, but he put a finger to her lips. "Please."

How could she argue with that? She nodded and pushed herself up. The room swayed, and Adam rushed to her side, helping her down the hall. When she slid under the covers, she gasped. "You changed my sheets?"

"Hush. You need a nap." He gently guided her shoulders back until she lay on the cool pillows.

Her eyelids drooped, and she found it hard to speak. "Mmkay." She snuggled down into the bed, relishing the feel of the clean sheets on her skin. Adam was amazing. She might be in love. Wait. Did she say that out loud?

The last thing she heard was Adam's chuckle as she drifted off to sleep.

CHAPTER 13

Megan continued to improve, although her cough lingered for a while. The next time she saw Adam, she tried to thank him for his kindness, only to have him wave it off. He seemed embarrassed she was calling attention to his good deed.

As she entered the station that Friday morning, her body tingled with anticipation. She tried to ignore it, but she had to admit, she was excited to see Adam. She walked down the hallway toward Leon's office, stopping when she heard tense voices.

"What do you think you're doing?" Adam's voice boomed.

"Chill, man. It's fine. I got this." Leon. What was that weasel up to now?

"You'd better. Because you know what will happen if…" His words were left hanging in the air.

"Don't worry."

Adam stormed out, almost running into her. His eyes widened. "Oh, sorry. I didn't know you were there."

"What was that about?"

He avoided her gaze. "Nothing."

"Didn't sound like nothing." She narrowed her eyes. What was he hiding? And just when she was beginning to trust him.

"Sorry." He shifted his weight. "Leon and I don't always see eye to eye. But he's the boss, ya know?" His eyes pleaded with her. "I don't always have a choice."

She studied him. Sweat formed on his forehead. She grabbed his arm. "What's he making you do?"

"Nothing." He pulled her down the hallway, away from Leon's office. "Just...no matter what happens, I'm on your side. Okay?"

What did that mean? And why did it sound so ominous? She nodded, unsure of what to think. Maybe he did want to tell her, and Leon was forcing his hand. Maybe this was all Leon's fault.

He glanced at his watch. "We'd better get on set. The show starts in a few minutes."

As Megan pinned her microphone on, she caught a glimpse of a woman off set wearing a beige business suit. Her heart caught in her throat. Doctor Lemon. Or whoever she really was.

Adam knew...that had to be what he wasn't telling her. Her mouth went dry. Why was the actress here? Was she going to reveal herself as a hack? What were they going to say?

She straightened in her chair, as Dale was already counting down. Nothing she could do about it now. If this was it and they were going to try to humiliate her, she was ready. She could deflect them.

After their first break, when they were supposed to introduce a teen violinist, Adam turned to the camera and flashed his plastic smile. "We've had a bit of a change in schedule. Tiffany Brighten was unable to make it today, so we've brought back a popular guest from earlier in the month.

Please welcome relationship specialist Doctor Shelby Lemon."

Megan kept her face passive, even after Adam shot her an apologetic glance. The girl posing as the doctor stepped up on the set and took a seat next to Megan. How had she not seen it before? The woman was quite young, only made up to look older with her over-sized glasses and an obvious wig.

"Tell us what you've been up to." Adam leaned forward, his television smile in place, but a bead of sweat belied his nerves.

Doctor Lemon laughed. "You know, the life of a researcher. Pretty boring. What I'd like, Adam, is to get an update on how things are going with you and Megan." She eyed the two of them over the rim of her glasses.

Adam chuckled. "Our relationship is an open book, Shelby. It's on the Internet, after all."

Megan's shoulders relaxed with relief. This was just an update show. They'd talk about their online dating, get more hype for Leon's website, and that would be it.

"Yes, of course I've been watching the show. Very entertaining. But what I'm most interested in is what happens off-camera." A wicked grin crossed Doctor Lemon's face.

Adam sat frozen, the stupid smile plastered on as if he'd stuck his face in cement. Megan jumped in. "Of course we speak to each other when we're not on camera, but you pretty much get to see everything important going on."

Adam snapped out of his stupor. "I'm curious to know what you think of our relationship, after watching our dates."

Yes. Turn the tables back onto her. Megan silently applauded him. The fake doctor patted his knee. "I have watched you grow closer. Is it true that your feelings for Megan have increased?"

He didn't miss a beat. "Yes. Most definitely."

"You get pretty cozy on camera. I'm glad to hear it's not

all an act."

Megan seethed, gripping the sides of her chair. Who was this fake to imply their relationship wasn't real, when she was the impostor? "We've grown quite fond of each other. Adam is a perfect gentleman."

"Well, not a *perfect* gentleman. I've seen those doorstep scenes." Shelby raised her eyebrows.

Adam laughed. "I've been told I'm a good kisser."

Heat rose to Megan's face, but she pushed down her embarrassment. It wasn't a lie. "I'm not going to argue."

"Why, Megan, you're blushing." The grin on Doctor Lemon's face gave her a sour stomach. "Tell me, how would you categorize your relationship with Adam?"

"We're friends." The words slipped out before she could think about them, but the look on Adam's face made her sink into her chair.

Doctor Lemon pursed her lips. "Surely you'll admit to being closer than *just friends*."

Megan cleared her throat, trying to buy time. What was she to say to that? Of course they were more than friends, if she were being honest with herself. But what should she call their relationship? There was no easy box to put it in. And it was none of *her* business anyway. "Yes, of course. I meant that I see Adam as a friend now, whereas before, I wouldn't have trusted him with a bag of Jelly Bellies."

He frowned, and the fake doctor appeared to be trying not to smile. "I do think you've come a long way. However, I think the two of you are hiding something. Is it true that Adam took you to meet his father on Easter Sunday?"

All color left Adam's face, and his jaw muscles flexed.

Doctor Lemon continued. "And is it also true that Adam was seen leaving your apartment Tuesday morning?" Her eyebrows wiggled in a suggestive manner.

Megan's hands shook, and she glared at Little Ms. Fake

Pants. "Like I said, Adam has never been anything but a gentleman."

"So, you don't deny it?"

All Megan could think about was punching the woman in the face. Adam spoke up. "I assure you, Doctor Lemon, our relationship is still in the beginning stages. We're getting to know one another, and I admit it's all thanks to you."

The good doctor turned her wicked smile on him. "Would you say your relationship has grown beyond friendship?"

Adam swallowed, glancing at Megan. "Yes."

"And would you admit to your fans that you would like to pursue a deeper connection?"

He paused. Megan didn't realize she was holding her breath until her lungs began to burn. Adam slowly nodded. "Yes."

"One last question." When had they lost control of the interview? "Are there going to be wedding bells in the future?"

Megan's mouth dropped open, and she had to sit on her hands to keep from ripping the woman's wig off her pointy little head. Adam shrugged and flashed his cool smile at the camera. "I guess our fans will have to watch to see."

After the show, Megan stormed into Leon's office. "Are you following me? Watching my apartment?"

Leon sat at his computer, his fingers making a clickity noise as they flew across the keyboard. "Mmm?" he asked, without turning to look at her.

Anger pulsed through her. She clenched her hands into tight fists. "Are. You. Following. Me?"

He looked up. "No. Your fans see you two. They talk. It's all on the website. There's quite a discussion going on about when Adam is going to pop the question."

"What?" Adam's deep voice sounded behind her, and she whirled around.

Leon frowned. "Don't you go on the website?"

"Yes. I print off all the comments each week." Adam folded his arms.

"No, not the comments, the forum." He clicked a few times, and they were staring at the Adam Warner and Megan Holloway forum. The most active thread was labeled, "Will there be a wedding?"

Megan's heart pounded in her chest. "What are you doing? You're encouraging these rumors, aren't you? I wouldn't be surprised to learn you started them."

A guilty look flashed across Leon's face and vanished just as quickly. "It's gaining viewers."

Her cheeks heated. "I am only going to say this once. I am not marrying Adam. I wouldn't marry him if I were dying and he was the only cure!"

"Hey!" Adam said, frowning.

She touched his arm. "No offense."

"How can I not take offense at that?"

A movement caught Megan's eye, and she turned to see Dale with his camera pointed at them. She let out a guttural yell and slapped her hand over the lens, shoving it back. "I can't believe you people!"

She stormed out of the station.

∞

A week after the Doctor Lemon fiasco, Megan was curled up on her sofa reading when her phone rang. The display read Adam. She couldn't stop the butterflies from acting up.

She slid her finger across the display to answer. "Hey."

"Leon just called me. He wants to see us down at the station right away, says it's important." Adam sounded breathless, like he'd been running.

The hairs on her neck stood. "What does he want?"

"I don't know, but we'd better get over there. Want me to pick you up?"

She glanced at the clock. "I don't know. It's getting late. What if people see us?"

He groaned. "Funny. I'll be there in a few."

"All right. But you'd better have me home before midnight, or people will talk." She didn't mean to be so sarcastic, it just came out.

She hung up, then decided to change out of her T-shirt and sweats and refresh her makeup. By the time he pulled up, she was ready and waiting for him. She slid into the passenger seat. "What's this all about?"

"Your guess is as good as mine."

When they got to the station, Leon was waiting in the lobby by the door. He pulled them inside and rounded on them. "ABC wants to buy the show."

Excitement shot through her. "What? How?"

Leon looked like a kid at Christmas. "I pitched our show and sent them tapes. They love the idea!"

Adam grabbed her arms and pulled her into an embrace. "ABC! Can you believe it? We're going to be on ABC!"

She hopped up and down with him, unable to contain her enthusiasm. "My mother's going to flip! She never thought I'd amount to anything in television."

Adam grinned. "And I'll be able to afford to bring my father to a closer facility."

"I can't believe we'll have our own morning show on a major network!"

Leon cleared his throat. "Um, no. It's nothing like that."

Somewhere in the back of her brain, she heard the horrible sound of a record player needle scratching over vinyl. "Wait. What are you talking about?"

Leon rubbed his mustache. "It's not your morning show

they want."

A cold lump formed in her middle. "What do you mean?"

"They want your dating show. They're going to bring on Doctor Lemon as the host, and the whole premise is Adam trying to win you over." His eyes gleamed. "They're making a whole mini-series, 'Winning Megan Over', or something like that. They're not sure of the title yet."

Megan's stomach lurched as her dreams went crashing into pieces. This was not what she expected. A major network...and all they wanted was to film her and Adam dating? That couldn't be right. There had to be more to it than that. "What would the show entail?"

Leon shrugged and shuffled his feet while staring at the plastic plant stuck in the corner of the room. "Um, well, not much, really. They want to show clips from our show. Give the readers a taste of what you guys are about. Then they'll have Doctor Lemon working with Adam, coaching him, helping him woo you."

She narrowed her eyes. "Woo me? Like, going on dates, right?"

"Yes. Dating will be part of it." His eyes shifted, and she could tell there was more to it.

"And what else?"

"I don't have to tell you that ABC is a major network. We are talking big money here."

Adam put his hands on his hips. "Leon..."

"This will be a huge jump for your careers. If this goes well, they will look at your morning show." He took a step back and hooked his thumbs in his pockets.

She was getting annoyed. "What else, Leon?"

"There's just one catch."

"What is it?" she and Adam said at once.

"They don't want it unless you agree to get married at the end of the show."

CHAPTER 14

Heat burned Megan's face, and she took a step toward Leon, her nose only inches from his. "I can't believe the depths of your greed."

He threw his hands up in surrender. "Hey, it's not me."

Megan poked his chest with one finger. "I don't believe that for a second. You pitched the show. You created the idea." She narrowed her eyes. "You came up with this scheme."

"You don't have to *stay* married."

Megan clenched her fists, her arms shaking with restraint. What she wanted to do was punch the guy.

Adam spoke up. "Wait. Let's take a second to—"

Megan rounded on him. "Don't you join his side. We are not getting married as some stunt for television. Not now, not ever." She wasn't going to be bullied into making herself a spectacle. And she was sure Leon planned on revealing Dr. Lemon as a fraud after the wedding, to humiliate her even more.

"They're paying each of you $100,000."

Adam staggered back. "A hundred grand?" His reaction mirrored her own. She couldn't believe it.

Leon grinned and shifted from one foot to the other. "I told you it was big bucks. They're prepared to push this show hard. Big advertising, big media events, you'll be on all the hot talk shows. You'll make names for yourselves."

"But not for our morning show." Megan saw her dream swirl and disappear into the drain. She didn't want to be some reality TV star. She didn't want to be known as 'the girl who married the chump and then found out his affections were based on a lie.'

Leon waved her comment away like a pesky fly. "You're not seeing the big picture. Once you're famous, you can write your own ticket. They give famous people talk shows all the time. Chevy Chase, Bonnie Hunt...even Magic Johnson got his own show."

Megan scowled. "Weren't all those canceled right away?"

"Bad examples. But that's beside the point. You know what being a household name can do for you. Think about it. Don't just say no because you're angry."

She glanced at Adam. He looked like a salivating dog. Of course. He wanted to advance his career, just like she did. And she knew how much it would mean to him to have his father closer.

What were the chances that Leon was right? If she made enough of a splash with this stupid facade, could she get her own serious show? She swallowed. It was possible.

Oh, but she loathed the idea of being the brunt of another one of Leon's cruel jokes. She'd had enough of that and couldn't bear to think of the humiliation. And not just local people would be watching this time. She'd be embarrassed on national television. A headache pounded in her skull. But Leon was right. Even if she was made the fool, if she handled it right, she might come out on top. And then maybe she could get her own show, away from Leon and Adam.

But...marrying Adam? She didn't want to sign papers and pledge to love him 'until death do us part.' Not if she didn't mean it. Marriage was sacred. At least to her.

She took a breath and let it out slowly. "Can't we do a fake wedding?"

Leon shook his head. "No. People dig into that kind of stuff. It has to be real. But the two of you don't have to really be in love. People marry all the time for reasons other than love. You only need to make it look convincing on camera." He chuckled. "And you're doing a great job of that already."

Probably because every stupid day she felt more attracted to Adam. Megan tried not to scowl. This was her own fault. She should never have agreed to go out with him. If she had refused, no one would be asking her to marry him.

And ABC wouldn't want her.

Thoughts of being on a major network sifted through her mind. Could she do it? Could she agree to marry Adam? She was attracted to him. And when he kissed her, the world spun. They had chemistry.

Adam and Leon stared at her, waiting for her to say something. Waiting for her to concede. Seconds ticked by as she tried to wrap her brain around what she was about to do. "When do they want to start taping?"

Leon's face brightened. "They want to have it on the fall schedule. They'll start taping immediately. But the last show, the wedding, they want to do live."

Live so they could embarrass her. She'd just have to think of a way to turn it on them. Make them look like fools. She turned to Adam. "What do you think?"

Several emotions played across his face before he spoke. "I think a hundred grand is difficult to turn down. I also think this could help both of our careers." He held up his hands. "But I don't want to force you to do anything you don't want to. I'll go along with it if you do, but if you say no, I'll back you up."

Leon coughed, and she could have sworn she heard the word 'wimp' in there somewhere. She tossed him a dirty look. "If I say yes, and that's a big 'if,' our marriage wouldn't be real, even if it's legitimate on paper. So, separate beds."

Adam squirmed. "Of course."

"And if I go through with this, we'll plan on getting a quiet annulment a few months after the show airs."

Adam nodded, a slight grimace crossing his features. "Sure."

Megan stared at the men, shocked at what she was about to say. Sighing, she plopped down onto one of the cheap lobby chairs and placed her head in her hands. "Fine. I'll do it."

Adam folded his arms across his chest, frowning. "Not exactly how I imagined a woman would accept my marriage proposal."

Megan tried to laugh at his levity, but all she could do was moan, already regretting her decision.

∼

Adam walked across the room, smiled at the camera, and sat on the plush leather seat. They had rented some swanky mansion to tape the show in, and all he could see were crystal chandeliers and gold accents shining from the bright film lighting. The infamous Doctor Lemon sat opposite him.

"Adam, before we begin, I'd like to ask you some questions regarding your relationship with Megan."

He nodded. "Of course."

"My analysis of you showed deep feelings for Megan, even before you started dating. Had you realized your feelings at the time?"

Great. Just what he wanted to do. Talk about his feelings on national television. Heat crept up his neck, and he adjusted his tie. "Um, no. I mean, I've always liked Megan. She's spunky. But I hadn't thought about her in a romantic way."

"And how has that changed?"

He squirmed and thought about the time he'd spent with her over the last few weeks. If he were being honest, he'd have to admit his attraction had grown. But what was he supposed to say on camera?

Doctor Lemon leaned forward and put her hand on his knee. "I sense your hesitation." She glanced around the room. "Ignore the cameras for a minute. Try to relax. We're just having a conversation."

Adam drew in a shaky breath and let it out. "Okay."

"You've spent the last few weeks dating Megan. How has that affected your relationship?"

"I've gotten to know her. We've become friends." He cringed at his own use of the word. That wasn't what he had meant to say.

Doctor Lemon peered at him over her glasses. "Now you're parroting Megan's words. Is it because you are afraid to admit you feel more for her than she does for you?"

"No. I mean..." He ran his hand through his hair. Was she right? He thought back to the times when he pulled her close, and caressed her soft lips with his. Was she only kissing him because of the camera? Did it mean more to him? "I do like Megan. A lot."

She pursed her lips. "If she were ill, would you stay by her side and nurse her back to health?"

Adam stared at the woman. Did she know? Was this a trick? He slowly nodded. "Of course."

"Would you be willing to put yourself at risk to save her, if she were in danger?"

He chewed his bottom lip. Of course he would. He couldn't bear to see any harm come to her. "I would."

"How far would you go? Would you risk death to save her?"

He imagined a situation where Megan was held at gunpoint, a man in a ski mask holding her throat. His gut clenched. What would he do? The answer came as his emotions surged. He'd run to her and pound that son-of-a-gun into the pavement. "Yes."

"Would you die to save her?" Doctor Lemon's voice was barely above a whisper.

His heart jumped into his throat and his pulse raced. He knew the answer. "Yes."

Doctor Lemon drew closer. "You love her."

The realization smacked him in the face, and he blinked. She was right. It had to be. Why else would he be willing to risk death for her? He slowly nodded.

Doctor Lemon turned a smug smile to the cameras. "I think we're ready to begin our first exercise."

~

Megan sat on a flimsy folding chair, back to back with Adam. Doctor Lemon—the faker—stood against a wall of books, directing some young crewmen to tie their arms together with rope. Two cameras fastened near the ceiling filmed them.

"Ouch, that's too tight." Megan squirmed.

The crewman winced. "Sorry. Is this better?" He loosened it a little bit, but not much.

"They need to be tight." Doctor Lemon folded her arms. "The point of this is to work together to get yourselves out of this situation."

After everyone left and the door was closed, Megan looked around. There was a small mahogany desk with a leather office chair, one lamp, and a wall filled with books. A large, expensive-looking rug took up most of the floor. "That's it? We're somehow supposed to work together to get untied? How are we to do that?"

One of Adam's low, sexy chuckles came. "I'm not sure."

"I can't hardly even wiggle my arms. Why'd they tie them so tight?"

"Probably so we don't cheat."

Megan blew out a breath. "Okay. Fine. But now what do we do?"

"Maybe there's a knife or a letter opener in that desk."

"Good thought. Do you think we can stand?"

Adam entwined her fingers with his. "If we push against each other."

"Okay." She tried to ignore the tingles his touch sent up her arms. "On the count of three." She counted, and they both pushed up. They managed to stand, but they were uncomfortably straddling their seats. "Let's go left. Ready?"

She took a step, only to realize Adam hadn't moved and it jerked him off balance. They teetered for a second, then toppled to the floor, Megan landing on top of him. A grunt came from underneath her.

"Oops! Sorry," she said, trying to peer over her shoulder at him. "You okay?"

"Fine," he choked.

She squirmed for a minute, trying to roll them over, but only succeeding in wiggling her backside up against his. Heat seared her face. "Um, I can't seem to get off you."

"No worries. I'm rather enjoying myself."

"Adam!" she squeaked. "You pig. Move!"

He sighed and rolled them into a sitting position. "You're no fun."

She held back a giggle. "We'll stand, then walk to the desk. Ready?" She waited this time, until he gave his assent. They pressed against each other, successfully standing. Moving toward the desk took a little more cooperation, but they were able to do so without falling.

They maneuvered around to the drawers and slid open the top one. "Empty." He didn't sound too disappointed, and Megan hid a smile. She had to admit this wasn't so bad after all.

They checked each drawer with the same results. "Now what?" She tried to blow a piece of hair out of her face.

"What's that on the shelf, over there?" He pointed to the far wall, where something silver glinted in the light.

They navigated to the other side of the room, where they found a pair of scissors on the shelf near where Doctor Lemon had been standing. "Ha! We did it." Megan grabbed them and slid her fingers through the handles.

"Now you can cut the ropes."

She angled several different directions, but couldn't get the scissors in the right position. "I can't. My hand doesn't bend that way."

Adam laughed. "Great. We did all that for nothing."

"And my arms are starting to go numb."

"Wait, I have an idea. You hold one handle, and I'll take the other. We'll point the scissors up, and see if we can cut through together."

His plan worked, and soon they had one arm free. Adam took the scissors and cut through the other rope, his fingers warm on her skin.

Megan smiled. "We did it!" She hugged him.

Doctor Lemon opened the door and shuffled into the room. "Well done. You passed your first exercise."

Adam cleared his throat. "What's the next one?"

Doctor Lemon smiled. "You get to meet your competition."

CHAPTER 15

Megan smoothed her black dress and nervously shuffled her feet as she walked down the dim hallway. When she entered the foyer, Doctor Lemon rushed over to her. "There you are. We're about to start. Come along, the men are waiting."

Her mouth went dry at the mention of 'the men.' When she signed up to do the show, she hadn't known she'd have to date other guys. And she wasn't sure what the deal was anyway. She'd signed a contract to marry Adam at the end. Why throw other men into the mix? It all seemed rather stupid to her.

But the producer was adamant. She was to flirt with these men and pretend she liked all of them. The audience couldn't know she was going to pick Adam at the end.

The sun had already set, leaving the backyard dark. The sliding glass door led to a large deck lit up with candles and tons of camera lighting. When she stepped out, all the air left her lungs. Three men who could easily be models stood leaning against the railing. Maybe this wouldn't be so bad after all. They were dressed in expensive suits and ties.

The first one had jet black hair and stunning blue eyes. He smiled at her and raised his glass of champagne. The second wore a cowboy hat, his broad shoulders and muscular physique displaying the hours he must work outdoors. The third held a rose and had longer hair, mussed up in a perfectly sexy kind of way. And then she noticed Adam. He was standing apart from the others, his eyes almost caressing her with his gaze. He smiled, his dimples causing her stomach to erupt in butterflies.

Doctor Lemon stepped forward and addressed the cameras. "This morning, Adam confessed his love for Megan."

The words sent a jolt of electricity through Megan. He did? She hadn't been allowed to watch Adam's interview. What had he said?

"Let's watch." Doctor Lemon motioned to a television mounted on the side of the mansion. Megan turned around and stared as Adam's face filled the screen. It was obvious the poor guy was nervous, and as the doctor pried him for personal information, he struggled to answer.

As the tape played, and Adam admitted he would risk his own life to save her, emotion swelled within her. She wanted to believe him. He looked like he was speaking from his heart. But he was also getting paid a hundred thousand dollars. She couldn't allow herself to be fooled. She steeled herself against the warmth surging through her.

Adam didn't love her. It was all an act.

After the clip with Adam, Doctor Lemon spoke. "As you can see, Adam feels deeply for Megan. Let's see if these feelings are returned."

A new tape played. This one was of Megan talking about how they were just friends. And then it skipped to her shouting that she'd never marry Adam, even if she were dying and he were the only cure.

Heat crept up her cheeks. That wasn't meant to be filmed. A couple of the guys chuckled, and Adam looked down at his feet.

She wanted to interrupt…to stop the obvious humiliation to Adam, but she couldn't. There was nothing she could say that would make it better. So she let it play out.

Doctor Lemon turned the television off and approached Megan. "Over the next few weeks, we will be doing some exercises to see if Megan is compatible with Adam." She looked around the deck. "Or if she might be better suited with another man." The cowboy tipped his hat to her, champagne dude lifted his glass, and the man with the mussed hair winked.

Megan gazed up into the night sky, hoping a stray boulder would fall on her. Or maybe the tail off an airplane.

With her hand on her hip, Doctor Lemon motioned for Megan to follow her off the deck. A stone bench sat between two large trees in the beautifully landscaped yard. "Here. Sit. It's time to meet the bachelors."

The first to be ushered over was champagne dude. "Heeeey," he said, stretching it out into two syllables. He ran his fingers through his perfectly styled hair. "I'm Anthony."

She felt like she should shake his hand or something, but he didn't offer it, so she just smiled and stuck her hands in her lap. "Hey."

He glanced around to find the camera. "So, I guess I'm, like, supposed to tell you about myself." He grinned, and his clear blue eyes made her stomach a little fluttery. "I'm a singer. Trying to make it, ya know. Be discovered. I tried out for The Voice, but that didn't work out, so I thought I'd get my foot in the door with something like this." He flashed her a smile, then she realized he was looking just over her left shoulder…at the camera.

She rolled her eyes and pushed down the urge to say, "I'm

over here, moron." Instead, she said, "What do you like to do in your spare time?"

"Play my guitar. Heeeey, maybe I can serenade you or something, huh? Show off my talent. Maybe woo you a little." He grinned like it was a brilliant idea.

Megan forced a polite smile. "Uh, huh."

The guy with the rose walked up. "Excuse me," he said in a thick French accent. "I think it is time to switch, no?"

Anthony frowned. "Already?"

"Oui."

With a groan, Anthony stood. "Okay, then. Have at her." He sauntered away.

The man sat on the bench and handed her the rose. "For you." His gaze traveled over her, and she suddenly felt shy.

"Thank you."

He took her hand and placed his other on top, enveloping it in warmth. "I'm Luc. And you are more beautiful than I imagined."

She cringed, wondering what he'd imagined. An image of an ogre with one eye popped into her head and she stifled a giggle. "Thanks."

"I am honored to meet you. Tell me about yourself."

She thought the men were supposed to do the talking, but she went with it. "I'm Megan. I co-host a morning show with Adam. I enjoy biking and running." She tried to come up with something else, but couldn't.

"Ah, you are athletic. I, too, do some running." He grinned and squeezed her hand. "Maybe we can go together sometime, no?"

His touch was sending little sparks through her, and she had trouble thinking. "Sure."

"And now a little about me. I was born in France, but came to America as a young man. I own a clothing store in upstate New York."

"Well, that's interesting." What else could she say about a clothing store? She searched her brain, but nothing came up, so she plastered on a weak smile.

"My days are full, but my nights are lonely." He picked up her hand again and kissed it, and the sweet moment turned uncomfortable.

"Well, Luc, that's very forward of you. We just met." She wiggled her hand from his grasp. "Probably not a good time to start talking about your lonely nights."

"Forgive me, madam." He was about to speak when someone cleared their throat behind him. The cowboy shoved his hands in his suit pockets.

Luc smiled. "It is time for us to part." He took her hand, kissed it once more, and then stood. "I shall see you later."

The cowboy watched as Luc walked off into the yard. "Well, isn't he smoother than a boar's behind?" He sat on the bench and stuck out his hand. "The name's Kyle."

Megan held back a laugh. "Nice to meet you."

He adjusted his hat. "I don't like to mess with pretenses, so here it is. I'd like to settle down and start a family. I've got a ranch out in Texas, worth a pretty penny. I'm just looking for someone to build a home with." He turned his dark chocolate eyes on her.

"I appreciate your honesty, Kyle." It was refreshing to find someone who said what they wanted, without any games.

"I'd like to get to know you, to find out if you're that someone."

She could already tell him the answer, but she kept that to herself and smiled instead. "Sounds like a plan."

He rubbed the back of his neck. "You ever been on a ranch, Miss Megan?"

"It's just Megan. And no, I haven't. What kind of ranch is it?"

"A horse ranch, ma'am."

"Oh." She knew about as much about horses as she did about rock climbing. Well, maybe even less since her date with Adam.

"Maybe we can go visit during one of our dates."

Was that possible? Would they fly her to Texas for a date? Even as she thought it, she knew they wouldn't bat an eye at spending the money to do something like that. She contemplated what it would be like to run off to Texas with Kyle.

The thought made her uncomfortable. What was she doing? She didn't even know these guys.

Movement behind him caught her eye, and Adam stepped out of the shadows. "I believe I get a turn now."

Relief flooded through her—and she had to admit, a little excitement. Kyle stood and shook Adam's hand, then departed with a wave. Adam slid onto the stone bench.

He glanced over his shoulder at the guys now milling about the yard. "They seem nice."

She remembered what the producer had said. "Sure," she said, trying to insert an air of noncommittal.

He grinned, his smile turning her insides into mush. "That good, huh?"

Megan hid a smile. Adam knew. "They're handsome." She raised an eyebrow, challenging him.

"Yeah, but can they do this?" He pulled her close, his lips probing hers with a kiss. Tingles shot over her skin, and her heart sped up. She closed her eyes and reveled in the feeling of Adam's kiss. It was stupid. She knew he was just playing it up for the camera. But she allowed herself to enjoy it anyway. When he pulled back, his gaze held something she couldn't quite decipher.

She smirked and lifted her chin. "We shall see."

Doctor Lemon emerged. "We're done for the night. We have a full day tomorrow, so get lots of sleep."

CHAPTER 16

Doctor Lemon tied a scratchy wool blindfold on Megan's head. "Can you see?"

"No."

"Good. Come with me." The woman tugged on her arm and led her through the house until Megan was turned around and had no idea where they were. The doctor suddenly stopped and placed her hands on Megan's arms. "Stay here. I'll send Adam in. He has the instructions. Your job is to trust him and do what he says." Her heels clomped on the hardwood floor, the sound fading as she walked away.

Megan stood listening to the distant churning of the air conditioner. Nothing happened for several minutes. She grew uneasy. "Hello?"

The door clicked and locked. Footsteps crossed the room. Megan smelled Adam's cologne right before he took her hands in his. Her sensations seemed heightened with the blindfold, and butterflies danced in her middle.

"Hey," he whispered.

She could barely breathe. "Hi."

His lips grazed hers, gently. Just a whisper of a kiss. Then he stepped back and let go of her hands. "You ready to get started?"

The kiss wasn't part of his instructions? Confused, she simply nodded.

"Walk forward three steps. You'll find a whiteboard. There are markers on the tray. Pick one up."

She did as she was told, holding out her hands until her fingertips touched the smooth surface of the board. She found a marker and uncapped it. "Okay."

"Draw a cat."

"Blindfolded? I can't even do that when I can see."

He chuckled. "Hey, I didn't make up the rules."

She blew out a frustrated breath of air. "Fine." She pressed the marker on the board and moved it around in what she hoped was the shape of a cat.

"Hmm."

"What? You going to make fun of my cat?"

"Looks more like an amoeba."

A giggle escaped. "Well, what do you expect?"

He came up behind her, his warm chest pressing against her back. "Let me help."

"Isn't that against the rules?"

"Nope." He put his hands on her hips and moved her over one step. Then he raised her arm. "Draw the number eight."

She complied, and he moved her hand to another spot on the board.

"Now draw a letter S." He continued to tell her simple letters and shapes to draw, moving her hand in place for the next one. His close proximity, along with the blindfold, was making it difficult to concentrate. Her knees were all wobbly.

"There." His breath was warm on her cheek, and it smelled of mint. "All done."

He lifted her blindfold so she could see her drawing. A

smile crept across her face. "Hey, that's not bad. It actually kind of looks like a cat."

Adam grinned, his dimples making her pulse race. "You're a regular Picasso."

She realized his hands were on her hips, his thumbs lightly stroking her. Why did his touch send her heart into overdrive? She knew he was just acting. Why did she let it get to her?

Doctor Lemon opened the door, a smirk on her face. "This trust exercise is done. You have passed with flying colors. Now it's time for Megan to have lunch with one of her suitors." She left.

Megan laughed and turned to Adam. "Suitors? Who says that anymore?"

He grinned. "The fifteenth century called. They want their word back."

She snorted, then covered her mouth with her hand, hoping the cameras hadn't picked it up. Adam just laughed at her and squeezed her hand. "Come on, you'd better go. Don't want to be late for your suitor."

It felt good to share a joke with him. With all the pretending going on, she enjoyed having something real between them.

∼

Megan took a bite of her sandwich and smoothed the picnic blanket. Luc leaned toward her. "You are so beautiful."

His French accent was sexy, but it was the fifth time he'd told her that, and she wasn't even to dessert yet. "Thank you." Maybe a change of subject would help. "Tell me, how long have you lived in New York?"

"Only four years. Before that, I studied business in Connecticut."

She stared at his high cheekbones and slightly mussed up hair. Quite sexy. Unfortunately, his talk of business bored her to death, and she had never been to the east coast. They had about as much in common as a walrus and a wiener dog. "Sounds interesting," she lied.

"Ah, not as interesting as you are beautiful."

Okay. That was getting uncomfortable. "Yeah, I think you said that before." She stuffed the rest of her sandwich into her mouth, hoping to hurry the date along. And maybe she'd look a little less beautiful with her cheeks puffed out like a chipmunk. Bonus.

He brushed a strand of hair from her face. "So many women are afraid to eat. I like that you're different."

She chomped on her food and tried to smile with her mouth closed.

"You're not afraid to be yourself," he continued. "You intrigue me." As he spoke, he leaned forward. She didn't realize his intent until his lips were on hers. His kiss was slobbery, and being as she hadn't swallowed all of her sandwich yet, she jerked back.

"I am sorry. Your beauty bewitched me."

Megan held up her hand while she forced the food down. She wanted to sock him one, but knew the producers would have a fit, so she smiled instead. "It's okay, Luc. I just wasn't ready."

His lips curled up in a devilish smile. "Maybe you are ready now, yes?"

She squelched the urge to make up an excuse. This was part of the game. She glanced at the camera. "Yes."

He came at her again. His kiss was more tongue than lip, and entirely too much saliva. She tried not to twist up her face in disgust. When he pulled back, she gave him a tight-lipped smile. "Mmm." What she wanted to do was wipe her mouth with the back of her hand.

He appeared to be pleased with her reaction. "I have been smitten with you, Megan."

"I *am* smitten with you," she said, correcting his grammar.

"You are?" He smiled.

"No. I mean…" How could she explain that one? She patted him on the hand. "Never mind."

After lunch with Luc, Kyle showed up for his date. He wore blue jeans and a plaid button-down shirt. When he saw her, he tipped his cowboy hat and smiled.

"I thought we could go riding." He stuck his thumbs in his pockets and rocked back on his heels.

"Riding…?" Megan wasn't sure what he meant. She didn't see any bicycles around.

Kyle grinned. "Horses, of course." He led her around the mansion and down a path to the stables.

"I didn't know this was here." She peeked into a stall, and a beautiful chocolate brown horse with a white star on his head stared back at her.

"I've spent the morning riding around the grounds and getting to know the animals. They are gentle and perfect for first-timers."

Megan turned to him. "Oh, I'm not a first-timer."

"You know how to ride?" His smile widened.

"Sure. I rode a pony when I was five years old at the county fair. Did a great job, if I do say so myself." A pained look crossed his face, and Megan laughed. "Kidding. I've ridden a few horses in my time, but it's been a while, so you'll have to remind me."

Kyle showed her how to get the animals ready for riding, putting on the saddles and making sure they were cinched up. Megan pulled on the leather strap, nervous the saddle would slide if it wasn't tight enough. He came up behind her. "Now, you don't want to cut the poor girl in half."

She spun around. "Did I hurt her?"

He chuckled. "No, you just don't want the cinch to be too tight. See, I can't fit my fingers in between. Let's loosen it a bit, but not so much that the saddle will spin."

After they were done, Kyle helped Megan onto her horse, a black beauty named Darksilver. "She's very tender. You shouldn't have any trouble with her, but if you feel insecure, just give me a holler."

Megan felt at ease with Kyle. He didn't mince words. Told things like he saw them. He was probably the most real out of all the guys, even Adam.

They rode down a trail in comfortable silence, the camera man trailing after them. Kyle led, but he frequently checked on how she was doing. She got used to the sway of the animal, although she knew she'd be sore if she were to spend a lot of time riding.

Kyle stopped his horse and dismounted. He walked over to her and helped her down. She looked around. "Where are we?"

He took her hand. "Come on, I'll show you."

His skin was rough, but not unpleasant. The hands of a working man. He was strong, and that made her feel safe. But the electricity that she normally had with Adam wasn't there.

He led her up a small hill to a precipice that overlooked the valley. She took in a sharp breath. "It's gorgeous."

"Would you like to sit for a while?" He indicated a large, gray rock jutting out from the earth.

"Sure." She climbed up and scooted over for him. A light breeze carried his cologne, not too overpowering, yet masculine. Nice.

He put his arm around her. "Nature has a way of healing your wounds, ya know?"

She looked out over the expanse, the lush green trees and the tiny roads cutting their way through. Birds chirped nearby. She knew what Kyle meant. "Yeah."

They chatted for a while about nothing important. Then Kyle rubbed the back of his neck and squirmed. "What made you do this show?"

Megan chewed her bottom lip. She couldn't tell him the truth, not with the camera man filming everything she said. She cleared her throat. "I guess I wanted to see what it would be like."

"How long have you known Adam?"

"Seven months. But we've only been dating for the past month." She picked at a piece of lint on her shirt.

They sat in silence for a few minutes before he scrubbed his face and said, "I don't really have a shot, do I?"

Megan stiffened. She wasn't supposed to let on who she was leaning toward. Granted, the whole show was about getting her to fall for Adam, so it wasn't going to be that big of a surprise, but she was supposed to go out with these guys and act like she could like any of them. Unsure of what to say, she just shrugged.

Kyle pulled his arm off her shoulders and hooked her chin with his finger so she had to meet his gaze. "I see the way you look at him. You love him, don't you?"

The words caught her off guard. She didn't love Adam. Did she? Thoughts of his smile invaded her mind. His touch made her insides turn to mush. She cared about him. Deeply.

Oh, dear heavens above. She was in love with Adam.

How did that happen? Adam didn't love her. He was just acting. This whole thing was a ruse, brought about by Leon and his stupid ideas. How could she have let her feelings go this far?

Kyle stared at her, his gaze imploring. She couldn't tell him. Instead, she stared down at her lap.

"I thought so," he said, his voice quiet. Maybe the camera didn't pick it up. He stood. "Let's go back. It's getting late, and you've got a dinner date with Anthony."

It killed her to see the sadness in his eyes. Out of the three, Kyle was the one she liked the most. But there was no chemistry.

After they got back to the stable and Kyle had the horses back in the stalls, he turned to her. "Thanks for going out with me. I think this is where I get off the train."

She jerked her head up in surprise. "You're leaving?"

He shrugged. "I'm about as useful here as a screen door on a submarine. Besides, I've got to get back to my ranch."

Megan wondered if Kyle quitting the show would make the producers mad. "Are you sure?"

A look of contemplation crossed his face, and he brushed his knuckles across her cheek. "No." He tipped her chin up and leaned down, pressing his lips to hers. It was like kissing her brother. Definitely a Princess Leia and Luke Skywalker moment. He stepped back and smiled, although it didn't reach his eyes. "Yes. I'm sure. Good-bye, Megan."

He left her standing in the stable.

CHAPTER 17

Kyle's announcement about leaving the show dampened Megan's spirits, but to say Anthony hadn't noticed would have been an understatement. He'd taken her for a walk around the gardens, his guitar slung across his back. He kept doing these weird dance moves as they walked, using them to punctuate whatever he was blabbering about at the time.

"Heeeey, I wrote you a song." He threw out his arms and shuffled his feet in what looked like an attempt at tap dancing.

She raised her eyebrows. "Really?" That explained the six-string on his back.

He swung his guitar around in what he probably thought was a cool move. "May I sing it for you?"

She actually debated telling him no, but in the end decided not to be rude. "Sure. I'd love to hear it." She sunk down on a wrought iron bench surrounded by little purple flowers.

Anthony grinned and then winked at her. No, wait. He

wasn't looking right at her. Good heavens, he winked at the camera. She slapped her hand to her forehead and leaned on the arm rest.

He strummed a chord. "Sweet Megan. Sweet, sweet Megan. You're like sunshine in the dark." Another chord. "Megan, sweet, sweet Megan, I want to take you to the park."

A laugh threatened to bubble up from her chest, but she suppressed it. Something told her it wasn't meant to be funny. He continued to sing, never quite hitting the high note, and always ending in a word that rhymed with dark. He managed to use mark, lark, stark, bark, snark, and even quark.

He ended the song with another dance move, and shot the camera a sexy smile. Megan wasn't sure if the song was about her, or about his love affair with being on television. She plastered on a polite grin and clapped. "That was very entertaining."

He bowed low. "It's what I do." Then he punctuated it with a twirl.

Megan stood, grabbed his arm and pulled him along the path. Maybe if they walked through the gardens and came out the other side, they'd be done with this ridiculous date. "What else do you like to do, besides play the guitar and dance?"

"I don't know, there's not much time to do other stuff, with all the gigs me and my band do." He turned a serious face to her. "Music is my life, man."

"People *pay* you to sing?" Right after the words left her mouth, she wished she could stuff them back in.

His face fell. "Well, sometimes. I mean, we've had a couple paying gigs."

"How do you afford your rent?" Again, she regretted her words. Why was she unable to filter her mouth today?

He shrugged. "My parents don't charge rent."

Oh, boy. She couldn't believe who they'd picked to try to woo her away from Adam. Luc, with his slobbery kisses and never-ending comments about her beauty, Kyle, who had walked off the show, and Anthony, a guy living in his mother's basement. Great.

She swallowed all the words stuck in her throat and simply smiled.

"But any day now the band will break out, and we'll make something of ourselves." He kicked a rock off the stone path. "I mean, this is a start, right?" He glanced at the camera.

How could she tell him his dream needed to die? That he'd never be a famous singer? She couldn't crush him like that. Instead, she changed the subject. "What do your parents think?"

His shoulders slumped. "My dad wants me to go into the family business. Says the money's more stable than chasing a pipe dream."

"What's your dad do?"

"He owns a heating and air conditioning company. He wants me to work for him, then eventually take over so he can retire."

It was obvious by his face he didn't like that idea. But singing would never work for him. She wished she could say something to persuade him to listen to his father. "Is heating and air conditioning that bad?"

His nose wrinkled like he'd kicked a skunk. "I've been helping him with his business since I was a kid and he could bribe me with a few dollars. It's boring, dirty work."

Megan twisted a strand of her hair around her index finger. "If you could pick anything in the world to do, besides singing, what would it be?"

"Why not music?"

"Let's pretend it didn't work out." She hoped he'd play along without further questions.

He looked up at the sky. "Modeling would be fun."

She clapped her hands together. "What a great idea! You'd be perfect for that."

He raised an eyebrow. "Really?"

"Yes! In fact, the first time I saw you, I thought you looked like a model."

An impish grin crept across his face. "That sexy, huh?"

She shoved him gently in the chest and laughed. "And humble, too." By this time, they'd finished their walk through the gardens, and Megan caught sight of Adam up on the deck of the mansion, a slight breeze blowing his hair. Her breath caught.

Anthony shoved his fists in his pockets and squinted at Adam. "You love him, don't you?"

She blew out a frustrated breath. What was up with everyone? Was it super obvious that she was a schmuck falling in love for real with a man who was only pretending? What a loser she was. But even as those thoughts swirled in her head, her pulse quickened when she saw Adam smile.

She couldn't answer Anthony, so she just played dumb.

"Well, he sure loves you. I can see it. And he said so."

What could she say to that? 'No, he's playing a part for television? He signed a contract?' She sighed and lifted one shoulder in a half-shrug.

His devilish smile made a re-appearance. "We should make your man over there a little jealous." He stroked her cheek with his thumb.

Apprehension overcame her. "I'm not sure that's a good idea."

"Sure it is." He came closer, his lips just a breath away. "Let's see how he likes this." And suddenly his mouth was on hers. Kissing Anthony was like an awkward teen kiss. Not unpleasant, but uncoordinated and over quickly. He smiled. "See. He's not too happy."

She glanced over at Adam, and sure enough, a frown had overtaken his face, his eyebrows drawn together. But, how was he supposed to react? The girl he confessed as his love was kissing someone else. If he kept smiling, he'd ruin the show. But she had to admit, a tiny part of her enjoyed his anxiety.

Megan put her hand on Anthony's shoulder. "Thanks for the date."

He pointed both index fingers at her. "You betcha." Then he twirled and did a little jig.

She couldn't help but laugh.

~

Megan twisted her fingers together as she sat on the leather straight-back chair. Doctor Lemon stared her down. Adam sat on the opposite side and seemed almost as nervous as she.

"Your next trust exercise will be in the form of a dinner date." The doctor looked like she was trying to hide a smile.

Megan released a breath she'd been holding. Eat dinner. She could do that. Easy peasy, right?

Adam nodded with a 'That's not so bad' expression on his face.

Doctor Lemon pulled out a small metal box with a hinged lid. "You will be driven by limousine to a fine restaurant. We'll give you time to change. There are new outfits in your rooms." She slid the box into Megan's hands. "The trust exercise comes when you open this box during dinner. There are instructions inside."

Megan clutched the cold metal container like it was about to come alive and wrestle her to the ground. She took a calming breath. Surely it couldn't be anything too horrible.

The doctor glanced at her watch. "You have a half-hour to get ready. You are dismissed."

Heart pounding, Megan stood and glanced at Adam. He raised an eyebrow at the box in her hand, but a smile slid onto his face. "This should be interesting."

Not the word she was thinking of. Leon, no doubt, was behind all of this. And he was the last person she trusted. "Yeah."

When she got to her room, she gasped at the black gown that hung on the back of her bathroom door. Silky, yet shimmering in the light, the cut both sexy and flattering. When she slid it on, it fit like it had been cut for her figure. She twirled in front of the mirror. Wow.

She freshened her makeup and ran a brush through her hair, then grabbed the metal box. Adam stood at the bottom of the grand staircase, leaning casually against the wall. When their gaze met, she sucked in a breath. She couldn't help it. He looked like he belonged in a men's fashion magazine. Or in a lineup at a wedding. Seeing him in a tux was doing strange things to her heart. As she neared, he winked at her and those dimples appeared. She broke eye contact and concentrated on not falling down the stairs.

He held out his arm. "There's a car waiting."

They stepped outside, to see a long stretch limo idling in the circular drive. She raised an eyebrow at him. "Car?"

He shrugged as the driver opened the door for her. "I guess Doctor Lemon wanted this to be a date to remember."

The silver box grew warm in her hand. "Yeah. I bet."

The restaurant was upscale, all white tablecloths and crystal wine glasses. They were seated in a secluded area so the camera men didn't bother anyone else.

Nerves assaulted her as she stared at the menu. "What are you getting?"

Adam seemed relaxed. "The halibut looks good. Their seafood is flown in fresh each day."

She snapped her menu shut. "Good choice. I'll have that, too." The reality was she didn't think she could eat anything before opening that stupid box, but she dreaded doing so.

After they ordered, Adam placed his hand on hers. "Do you want to open it, or keep staring at it like it's going to bite you?"

She tore her eyes from the silver lid. She had to know what was in it. Then maybe she could get it over with and enjoy the rest of the date. "You open it."

He picked up the metal container and flipped up the lid. It appeared to be filled with small strips of paper. His gaze flickered to hers before he read the instructions. "Take turns selecting and following the directions on each piece of paper. You must use them all." He set the box between them, then eyed her. "Want to go first?"

She shook her head.

He grinned, then picked up a white strip and smoothed it out on the table. "Tell your date about your most embarrassing moment."

Relief flooded through her. That wasn't so bad.

Adam chuckled and tossed the paper in the middle of the table. "Okay, it has to be the time I accidentally called our fifth grade teacher her nick-name…to her face."

Megan held in a giggle. "Do tell."

"Ms. Starkbaum was the math teacher. Except everyone called her Stink Bottom. When she called me up to the board, I said, "Yes, Ms. Stink Bottom." Of course, the entire class erupted in laughter, and I got detention."

"You poor thing."

"Yeah, wasn't fair at all. Everyone called her that. I just slipped up in front of her."

Megan bit her lower lip. "Mine was in middle school."

He raised an eyebrow and his dimples appeared. "Can't wait to hear it."

"My gym bag's zipper had broken. It wasn't a big deal until I dropped it on the cement and my clothes dumped out. My underwear caught a breeze and flew across the school parking lot."

A pained look crossed Adam's face. "Ooh, that's bad."

"I wish that was the worst of it. Billy Holt caught them and proceeded to show everyone where my mother had written my name on them."

It was obvious he was trying not to laugh. "Yeah. That's worse." A snort erupted and they both laughed.

He nudged the box toward her. "Your turn."

"Oh, all right. That one was a freebie." She reached in and grabbed the first paper that touched her fingers. "Share your earliest betrayal."

Adam froze, his gaze flickering to the camera. Without a word, she understood. He was glad she had gotten that one. There were some things he didn't want to share in front of America.

She cleared her throat. "That's easy. First grade. I was best friends with Erin Williams. A new girl moved in. Shelly Fry. A cutie with red curls all down her back. Erin hated her, but I wanted to be friends. I convinced Erin she wasn't so bad. The next week, I came to school and they were talking about me behind my back. All of a sudden, Erin and Shelly were best friends, and I was left out."

Adam scoffed. "Girls are so fickle."

She opened her mouth in mock indignation. "Hey, don't blame our entire gender. It was Erin's fault."

"She missed out." His words were light, but his eyes darkened and his face turned serious.

She pushed the box toward him. "All yours."

He reached in and grabbed one. "Tell your date the thing you fear the most." A look crossed his face, but vanished before she could put a name to it, and a smile replaced it. "Easy." He took her hand, warmth spreading through her. "Losing you."

CHAPTER 18

Adam hadn't meant to make a joke out of it, but he could tell by Megan's face that's how it came across. She scrunched up her nose and pulled her hand back. "Fair enough. I guess it's my turn again."

He'd made her mad. Stupid. Why did he always fall back on that fake macho persona Leon pushed on him? Regret filled him.

She reached into the container, shuffling around the strips before selecting one and uncurling it. "Reveal your deepest secret."

Her face drained of color, and he instantly felt bad for her. Nothing like revealing your deepest secret on national television. Trying to keep the mood light, he said, "This should be interesting."

She narrowed her eyes. "That's easy. Everyone already knows I'm secretly in love with my co-host." She scrunched up the paper into a tiny ball and tossed it over her shoulder. "Next."

The question had gotten to her, obviously. But she successfully side-stepped it. Maybe they could get this game over with if they went quickly. This time he drew from the bottom. "Name one thing you always wanted for Christmas, but never got."

He lifted his gaze to meet hers, and saw compassion behind her eyes. He couldn't answer this truthfully, either. Not with the cameras rolling. So he picked something out of the air. "Probably what every kid wants. A pony." He flashed a fake smile.

"Me too. Why does every kid want a pony? They're a lot of work to take care of."

"Kids don't think about the work. Only the fun." He placed his hand on her arm.

"Too bad the fun only lasts a short time, but the work goes on." She stared at his hand until he removed it. "I guess it's my turn again."

After silently reading her paper, a smile crossed her face. "If you could dare your date to do one thing, what would it be?"

"Hey, that's not fair. This is supposed to be about sharing."

Her brow arched. "It's a trust exercise. Don't you trust me?"

"Not with that devilish look on your face."

Her laughter carried through the room. "Hey, the paper only asked what I would dare you to do. It didn't say you had to do it."

He wiped his brow in pretend relief. "Good. Because I haven't forgotten the karaoke contest."

"You weaseled your way out of that, if I remember properly. Got a standing ovation."

"I have mad skills." He gave her a sexy grin, and she blushed.

"Okay. Your dare would be..." She looked up at the ceiling for a moment. "To spike your hair in a mohawk."

"That's it?"

"And wear it on our morning show."

He laughed. "You know how to dare."

A smug look formed on her face. "You are talking to the reigning champion of the sixth grade truth or dare tournament."

They continued to take turns with the box, a silent understanding passing between them to evade the questions they didn't want to answer on the air. When their food arrived, they only had two pieces of paper left.

Adam motioned to the box. "I guess these will have to wait."

A frown crossed Megan's face. "No way. I'm getting this over with so we can enjoy the rest of our date." She pulled out a paper and uncurled it, then grimaced. "Share your most painful childhood memory."

The display of emotion that played out on Megan's face brought out a desire in him to protect her. She shouldn't have to talk about things like this in front of millions of people. What right did Leon have to do this? He was about to say something, but she smoothed out her features and smiled. "Probably the time I crashed my bike and skinned both knees. Took a week to heal." She crumpled the paper and pushed the box toward him. "Last one's yours."

He took the paper and unfolded it. "Tell your date about your first kiss." He groaned and tossed the paper into the pile in the middle of the table. "Of course, it had to be that."

"What? It can't be that bad."

He sucked in a breath and leaned back in his chair. "I'm afraid it is."

"Well, you can't stop there. You have to spill it."

"Okay. I was in third grade. My best friend Jeffery dared me to kiss Emily, the prettiest girl in class. I told him I wouldn't do it, but then he double dog dared me to." He kept his face straight to show the seriousness of the situation.

"Oh, no. You can't back away from a double dog dare." Megan picked up her water and took a sip. "What did you do?"

"Of course I had to do it, or forever be branded as a coward."

"Naturally."

"So, during recess I told Emily there was a cool frog out behind the school. She didn't seem interested." He shrugged. "I guess girls don't like frogs. Who knew?"

Megan snorted. "You really thought that would work?"

"What can I say? I was eight. When I changed it to a kitten, she perked up. She followed me, even though we weren't allowed to leave the playground."

A smile tugged at Megan's lips. "You rebel."

"I definitely was. And after we got out back, and there was no kitten, Emily turned to leave, and I panicked. I said the first thing that popped into my head."

"Which was?"

He bit back a grin. "I double dog dare you to kiss me."

Megan giggled. "Not very original, were you?"

"Nope. But it worked. She stopped, turned around and looked at me for a moment, like she couldn't decide if she was going to do it or not."

"She must have, since this is the story of your first kiss." Megan's eyes twinkled.

"You're right. She took two steps toward me, and said, 'Okay.' Then she closed her eyes and puckered her lips. I planted one on her so fast, she probably thought I socked her. Then I turned to see Mrs. Zuckerman and the entire fourth grade English class lined up along the windows, watching us."

Megan laughed. "No way! What happened?"

"We got in trouble for leaving the playground. But good

thing it happened back then. Today I'd have been charged with sexual assault."

"Sad, but true." Megan picked up her fork and stabbed a piece of asparagus. "Well, your story beats mine."

Curiosity piqued in him. "Fess up."

She chewed, then swallowed. "It's boring compared to yours."

"Too bad. You have to tell it now."

"I was sixteen, and on my first date. Harry Davis. A skinny kid with freckles." She picked up her water glass. "He kissed me on the doorstep after the date."

"That's it?"

"Told you it was boring." She smiled, then took a sip of her water.

"What a letdown."

She glanced at the camera. "Remind me to tell you sometime about my second kiss. Much more entertaining."

The gleam in her eye made him chuckle. "You got it."

∼

Megan punched the pillow in her mansion room and rolled over...again. Why was she so restless? That stupid trust exercise had her stomach all tied up in knots. What was Leon thinking, that they'd really share all that personal stuff on national television? He had some nerve.

Her stomach growled, and she looked at the clock. Three fifteen. The halibut had been delicious, but not as filling as she'd hoped. And since she had no chance of falling back asleep anytime soon, she slid out of bed and pulled on her robe. Maybe there was something in the kitchen she could snack on.

The hallway was dark, only lit by a sliver of moonlight

shining through a small decorative window high on the far wall. She padded down the back staircase and through another hall that led to the kitchen. The cold tile reminded her she'd forgotten to put on slippers.

She opened the refrigerator, and the bright light hit her in the face. She was standing there blinking, staring at the blurry contents, when a voice behind her made her jump.

"Looks like I'm not the only one who couldn't sleep."

She squealed and turned to face Adam, who wore flannel pajamas and a smirk on his face. "Adam! You scared me."

"Sorry. Didn't mean to startle you." He took a step toward her, his hair tousled in a sexy bed-head way. "Anything good in there?"

She turned back around, her heart hammering in her chest, not entirely from alarm. "I don't know. My eyes hadn't adjusted yet."

He grabbed the door and opened it wider, his body now so close she could sense his warmth. "Hmm. Grapes?"

She shook her head. "No. Middle of the night snacks shouldn't be healthy."

A chuckle came from behind her. "Pudding?"

She peered into the light, still unable to see anything. "What flavor?"

He reached past her and grabbed something. "Looks like chocolate fudge."

"Now you're talking."

He chuckled again, and his breath brushed her cheek. Smelled like mint. What did he do, chew gum in his sleep? He handed her the cup and grabbed another for himself. "Okay. Chocolate pudding it is."

She closed the fridge and turned to find Adam hadn't moved, effectively pinning her to the door. She looked up at him. For some reason he was staring at her with such intensity, she could barely breathe. She stood frozen as the seconds ticked by, his lips so close to hers she could almost taste them. But he blinked and moved back, and the moment evaporated like mist in the sun.

They pulled open drawers until Megan found the spoons. When she handed Adam his, their fingers touched and electricity zapped through her.

Dang. She'd better get away from him. Being alone like this was not a good idea. Not when she couldn't trust her treacherous body.

She leaned against the counter and opened her container. The pudding was cold and had the perfect amount of chocolate. She let it slide down her throat and soothe her nervous stomach. She clutched the cool cup and dared a glance at Adam.

He stood staring at her, almost like he wanted to speak but was holding back. She frowned. "What?"

"Nothing. I was just thinking about our trust exercise."

She rolled her eyes. "Yeah, wasn't that fun?" She adopted a nasal voice, mimicking Doctor Lemon. "Tell everyone your deepest, darkest secrets. It will be good for you."

He laughed. "You do a pretty good impression of her."

Megan curtsied. "Thanks."

Adam's face grew serious again. "You know, I never wanted a pony."

She stared at him, her throat tightening. "Yeah. I figured."

He leaned back on the counter, crossing his feet at his ankles and pushing the pudding around in his cup. "The only thing I wanted was to be with my dad again. I didn't understand why Santa wouldn't give me that."

She slid closer to him and put her hand on his back. "I'm sorry. How awful for you."

He shrugged. "I grew up. Learned the ways of life. Found out Santa wasn't real, and that sometimes no matter how hard you wished for something, it wasn't going to happen."

"That's a hard lesson for a kid."

"It was." He sighed and stared at his pudding. "I'm just thankful I have my father in a better facility." Then he turned his ice blue eyes on her. "I appreciate you doing this."

Guilt worked its way into her. The only reason she was doing the show was to advance her career. And even then, she'd almost refused. She hadn't wanted to agree to a fake marriage, something that now paled in importance. "Sure," she muttered.

He swallowed, then shifted his weight. "Can I ask you something?"

"Okay."

His gaze bore into hers. "What were you thinking of when you were asked to share your deepest secret?"

Her chest tightened, and a chill ran over her skin. For a moment, she thought about blowing off the question, but an urge to tell him surged in her. She broke the eye contact and stared at her feet, unsure of how to begin.

"I'm sorry. I shouldn't have asked."

"No. It's okay. I've just never told anyone before. It's kind of hard."

He nodded and waited for her to continue.

She took a deep breath. "When I was six, a girl in my town was kidnapped. They found her body three weeks later, in a creek." She raised her gaze to stare into his eyes. "I could have prevented it."

His eyebrows knit together. "How?" he asked, his voice soft.

She set the empty pudding cup on the counter and folded her arms across her chest. "Two days before her kidnapping, I was playing outside in my yard. A man pulled up in a van, saying he'd lost his puppy. I knew better than to go near a stranger, but he seemed so worried. I wanted to help. The next thing I knew, he grabbed me and pulled me toward his van."

Adam took in a sharp breath. "That's horrible."

"I was able to wriggle out of his grasp. I ran into the house and hid under my bed until Wendy came looking for me. I was so scared I'd get in trouble, I never told anyone. Then when the other girl turned up missing, I locked it up in my head and convinced myself to forget it ever happened." Her hands shook, and she twisted her fingers together.

He pulled her close, his strong arms enveloping her, wrapping her in warmth. "It wasn't your fault," he whispered into her hair.

She trembled, unable to stop. "I know, but if I had said something…" Her vision blurred.

He pulled back, his gaze intense. "You were only six years old. You probably couldn't even have given them the license plate number." He brushed a tear off her cheek with his thumb.

Megan blinked as she processed that thought. "You're right. I didn't think of that."

He hugged her again, tucking her head under his chin. "You were so young. It's very possible your account of the incident wouldn't have stopped the man. You can't hold yourself responsible."

For the first time, Megan allowed the guilt to subside. And while she stood in the kitchen, wrapped in Adam's warm embrace, she finally felt at peace.

CHAPTER 19

Megan stepped back, suddenly embarrassed to be so close to Adam while wearing her silky robe and pajamas. She hadn't meant to cling to him like Saran Wrap. She raked a shaky hand through her hair. Changing the subject would be good. "Can I ask you something?"

"Sure."

"What was your earliest betrayal?"

Emotion played across his face, and he swallowed. He seemed to search for words for a moment. "Well, Mom leaving us, but I was too young to understand that. Later, I had a foster brother in one of my placements, Nathan. Something wasn't quite right with the kid. I think his parents thought having another child around would be good for him."

She nodded, silently encouraging him to go on.

"He acted like my friend, at first. He had a huge collection of Hot Wheels, and we'd spend hours playing with them on the basement carpet. The family had a pet dog. Beautiful collie named Butch. I loved that dog. I think Nate was jealous. One day I came home from school and Butch was lying on the front porch. At first I thought he was sleeping, but as I approached I saw blood. He'd been stabbed. A lot."

Her stomach lurched, and her hand flew to her mouth, covering a gasp. "Nate did that?"

"Yes. They moved me to another family after that."

"I'd hope so."

"Last I heard, Nate was in jail for armed robbery."

She nodded, unsure of what to say. "Wow." She'd known he'd had a rough childhood, being ripped away from his father and put into foster care, but she'd had no idea it was that bad. What a traumatic event. The thought jumped in her head to pull him close, but she pushed it away. Instead, she put her hand over his.

He slid his other hand over hers, and squeezed. An unspoken communication passed between them. It was as if he understood why she was holding back, and accepted it. They stood for a few seconds, a feeling Megan couldn't quite place coming over her. After a moment, Adam pulled his hand back.

"Okay. Your turn. Most painful childhood memory. Can't be scraping your knees."

"You're right. All my painful memories have to do with my mother. She's the one with the temper in our family."

"Did she hit you?" he asked, quietly.

Megan shook her head. "No. But she threw things. Screamed at me. Told me I was no good. I wasn't really thinking of a single incident. Life was better when she was at work, which was a lot of the time, so I was glad for that."

"And your dad?" His tone was soft. Understanding.

"He always smoothed things out between Mom and me. We had a good relationship." She blinked back sudden tears. "I miss him."

"You don't get to see him much?"

She shook her head. "No." She could have gone into greater detail, but left it at that. With her mother being the way she was, it was difficult to spend time with her father. She forced a smile. "Okay, what about your biggest fear? It's definitely not losing me."

He chuckled, and she realized she liked the sound. It rumbled in his chest, making her pulse jump. "What, you don't think I care about you?"

She smirked at him. "You weren't thinking that, and you know it. Come on, spill."

"All right. My biggest fear is probably having Leon make a mockery of my father on national television." A smile formed on his lips, and he put his arm on her back, sending warmth and tingles through her. "But don't sell yourself short. You've grown on me. I mean, I'm going to propose soon, you know."

She froze, the warmth she'd felt a moment ago turning cold. Of course, she knew he was only doing it for the show. And it wasn't real. But the thought of him proposing sent shivers through her anyway. "When?" she asked, her voice breathy.

A devilish look gleamed in his eye. "Now, I can't tell you that. It has to be a surprise." He moved closer to her, bending low. She couldn't take her eyes off his lips. Why did she have this sudden urge to kiss him? The pull was almost overwhelming.

She glanced away to break the spell. "Well, I guess I'd better head to bed. I've got a date with Luc in the morning."

"Ah, poor man," Adam said in a bad French accent. "He will lose at this game of love."

She tried not to laugh, but a giggle escaped anyway. "You shouldn't try to speak in an accent. You might hurt yourself."

His grin widened. "Or maybe it's just too sexy."

She poked him in the side. "You better get to bed. You're

delusional from lack of sleep." As she left the room, she heard him chuckle.

CHAPTER 20

The next three days were spent going on outings with Luc, Anthony and Adam. Every interview with Doctor Lemon grew tenser, with the fake doctor pushing Megan to admit she was in love with Adam. No matter how many times she told herself it was only a television show and she'd signed a contract and she needed to say the words, she still couldn't force them through her lips.

While she readied for another date with Adam, she blew out a frustrated breath. It wasn't like she didn't feel anything for him. She did. Too much, really. He didn't love her. He was acting, so why did she get butterflies every time she saw him? And why couldn't she just do some acting of her own? Tell Doctor Lemon she loved him?

The answer hit her like a sucker punch. She couldn't say it because she was afraid it was true. Saying it would only reaffirm what she feared. She had fallen in love with Adam. Would Doctor Lemon be able to see it?

She shook her head, not believing what was going through her mind. Doctor Lemon was a fake! She wouldn't know a relationship from a monkey's rear end. Of all the things she should be worrying about, Doctor Lemon finding out she was really in love with Adam was not one of them.

She slipped into her sun dress and sandals, and finished applying her makeup. The stupid fake doctor was going to get what she wanted in this after-date interview. She'd confess her love for Adam. They were paying her a hundred thousand dollars. She had to go along with it, right? No one needed to know her true feelings.

Having made the decision, her nerves grew into a tangled mess. Maybe she could put that out of her mind for her date. Ignore the uneasiness making her stomach clench. She stared at herself in the mirror. Who was she kidding? She was going to be a nervous wreck.

On the way out of her room, she grabbed her clutch purse. She expected to see Adam waiting in the entryway, but it was empty. The camera man followed her as she wandered around the main floor, growing more confused as she went. When she couldn't find anyone, she stepped out onto the back deck.

Doctor Lemon sat on the wooden bench. A smile quirked her lips before she smoothed it out. "A car is coming for you and Adam. Please go pack your bags."

Panic closed Megan's throat, and she forgot all about having to confess her love. "What? Are we being kicked off the show?"

Megan got the distinct impression Doctor Lemon was trying not to laugh. "No. You are going on a date. You'll be spending the weekend on a romantic beach in Florida. We've booked two rooms for you at a five-star resort."

Relief flooded through her a second before the realization hit. This was it. This was when Adam would propose. Of course they'd do something extravagant like this. She tried to smile and show a little enthusiasm for the surprise getaway. "Wow. That's…great."

Why had she agreed to do this? Her acting skills obviously stunk. And now the nerves inside her had grown big enough to have little baby nerves to terrorize her. She flashed one last pathetic smile toward Doctor Lemon and fled to her room.

She tossed some things in her suitcase. In all honesty, she wasn't paying much attention. Hopefully she wouldn't get there and realize she'd only packed shirts. She threw in her makeup kit and zipped her rolling case, then proceeded to drag it down the stairs. This was going to be a nightmare.

Adam stood by the front doors, his travel bag by his feet. Seeing him made her nerves run rampant. He looked up at her, and a hint of a smile played across his features. "Hey."

Why was he so good looking? Why did her heart have to pound like she'd never seen a handsome man before? She gripped her case and took the remaining steps toward him. Oh, dear. He smelled good. "Hi."

"I guess they're sending us to a resort." He turned away. She'd have thought he was acting shy if she didn't know him better.

"Yep." Had she packed her swimsuit? She wasn't sure. Didn't matter. No way was she going swimming with Adam. Better to stay away from wearing skin-tight barely-there things around him.

He stared out the tiny window. "Have you ever been to Florida?"

"Hmm?" His words took a second to register. "Oh, no." Her fingers tingled and felt numb. Was it possible to lose the feeling in your extremities because of stress? Could nerves do that? She stared down at her hands, twisted into a tight knot. Oh. Maybe she was just strangling the blood right out of them. She shook her hands and let out a breath.

"They're here." Adam picked up both their bags and still managed to open the door for her. "After you."

It wasn't a limousine this time, just a regular taxi. The driver was chatty, and Megan was thankful the camera man wasn't with them. A few of the crew had already flown out so they could set up at the resort.

When they got to the airport, they boarded a private jet. Megan decided she could get used to that. No long lines, far less waiting, and luxurious accommodations. They even had champagne, although she didn't drink any. Her nerves were making her nauseous.

The clock read six thirty-five when they touched down in Florida. Adam grabbed her hand and pointed out the small airplane window. "Look at the sunset."

Of course the sky was gorgeous. He was gorgeous. The stupid plane was gorgeous. And she couldn't enjoy a second of it because she knew what was coming.

~

Megan took a small bite of her shrimp. She'd been pushing her food around her plate for the last half hour. Adam had finished and was staring at her with this weird expression on his face. Was he about to pop the question?

Worrying about when he was going to ask was ruining everything. She needed to get a grip. There'd be no enjoying the weekend if she couldn't get past the proposal. She set her fork down and took a cleansing breath.

"You seem tense." Adam placed his hand over hers, and she jumped, and a completely embarrassing squeak came out.

Heat seared her face, and she hoped the microphone hadn't picked that up. "Uh, yeah. I guess. Sorry. I'm not used to hopping on a plane and flying off to some island resort."

"It is a little weird." He chuckled, his dimples turning her nerves into butterflies.

The camera man walked around the table to get a better angle on her, and she tried to ignore him. She stared off the patio at the expanse of darkening sky over the tide coming in. The light breeze carried the scent of seaweed and salt water, and a hint of Adam's cologne. Her gaze fell on him.

Was he going to propose tonight? They'd just arrived. Surely he'd wait until they were more settled. Right? It was too early to do it. She studied him, trying to gage his thoughts.

"Listen, Megan..." He squirmed in his seat as his voice trailed off.

Oh, crap. This was really it. He wasn't going to wait after all. And she hadn't even confessed to Doctor Lemon that she loved him. Would it be unrealistic for her to accept a proposal if she'd never even admitted that she loved him?

He took a breath to continue, and she panicked. "I love you," she blurted. Unfortunately, the force of her words caused a blob of spit to fly out of her mouth and land on Adam's cheek.

Mortified, she stared at the saliva slowly sliding down his face. Should she apologize and wipe it off? Ignore it? Her throat closed. Ignore it or wipe it?!? What should she do? Maybe he hadn't noticed. She wasn't sure if the stunned look on his face was because of what she said, or the ball of slobber leaving a wet slug-like trail down his skin.

"You, um...what?" He picked up his napkin and subtly patted his cheek. "Say that again?" A sexy half-smile formed on his face.

Relieved when he didn't call attention to the fact that she'd spat on him, but rather successfully dealt with it without being obvious, she giggled. It came out high pitched and hysterical. Now she felt silly for confessing her love. Maybe he really hadn't heard her. "What did I say? I'm not sure. Who knows?"

His grin grew, and his gaze flickered to the camera. "You said 'I love you.'"

A blush warmed her face. "Did I?" No getting out of it now. She had to go with it. "I mean, yes. Yes, I do."

He raised his eyebrows.

She took a deep breath and let it out slowly. Maybe getting this whole thing over was best. Rip it off, like a Band-Aid. "I love you. So, if you have something you want to tell me, go ahead."

He blinked, his face blank. "What?"

"You were going to say something before I interrupted. Sorry. Go ahead. I'm ready now." She waved her hand to encourage him to get on with it.

His lips twitched, like he was trying to hide a smile. "I was just going to ask if you wanted to call it a night. You look tired."

Really? That's what he was going to say? She swallowed, her mouth suddenly dry. "Oh." She picked up her glass and took a big gulp. Her hand shook so bad she almost slopped water all over the table.

"You seem to have been thinking I was going to say something else." The corners of his eyes crinkled in a hidden smile.

"Nope." She set her glass down. The warmth in her face spread until she was sure she looked like she'd had an allergic reaction to the fish. "Not at all."

He seemed to be enjoying her discomfort way too much. "I see. Maybe before we head back to our rooms, we should take a romantic stroll along the beach." He stood, grabbed her hands, and pulled her up on her wobbly knees. "I think there's something we should probably discuss."

Oh, this was it. He really was going to propose now. She tried to calm her thudding heart as she walked alongside him to the water's edge. "All right." Her voice came out breathy and weak.

They walked through the sand, the camera men trailing behind them, and Adam's thumb rubbing slow circles over the back of her hand, driving her crazy. The beauty of the moonlit beach provided the perfect setting. Any minute now he would get down on one knee.

Adam stopped and wrapped his arms around her, pulling her close to his muscular chest. "You look beautiful tonight," he whispered into her hair.

Her pulse raced, and she fought to keep control of her head. "Mmm. Thanks."

Adam leaned down and kissed the spot below her earlobe, and she swooned. Come to think of it, she wasn't sure how a person would do that, but she couldn't think of any other word for it. He kissed her jaw line, then brought his lips to her ear. "Doctor Lemon gave me one last trust exercise to do while we're here."

Her heart pounded in her ears so loudly, she could barely hear him. "What is it?" she asked, breathless from what his kisses were doing to her.

He grinned. "You'll find out." He tucked her arm into the crook of his elbow and began walking them back to the resort.

The dirty rat. He knew she was expecting the proposal. He knew exactly what she would be thinking. And he was toying with her.

She glared at him, and all he did was chuckle in response.

This was going to be a long weekend.

CHAPTER 21

Adam knew exactly why Megan looked like she was going to throw up as they boarded the plane. She'd guessed the purpose of the trip, and it obviously scared her to death. After the first misunderstanding, he decided to make a game out of it. Before breakfast he wadded up a napkin and stuck it in his shirt pocket, making it look like a ring box bulge. Every time he patted his pocket, Megan's face blanched. When he finally reached in and took out the napkin, her wide eyes narrowed and the familiar 'I'm going to kill you' look came into her eyes. But then she relaxed, and a hint of a smile played on her lips.

As they walked along the pier, he knelt down on one knee, only to tie his shoe. She laughed at that one, and relaxed even more. By dinner, she was back to her old self, carrying on normal conversations and throwing her usual zings his way when he got under her skin. That was when he decided it was time.

The setting sun set the perfect backdrop. A light breeze blew as they sat on the deck of the restaurant and ate the most amazing grilled seafood. Megan sat back in her chair, staring at the streaks of pink and orange that lit up the sky.

He leaned forward and took her hand. "Megan, dating you has been an experience like no other." A suspicious look passed over her face, but she replaced it with a smile. "From fine dining off the kid's menu, to surprise karaoke, I never know what I'm going to get with you."

Her smile turned into something more akin to a smirk, and she appeared to be biting the inside of her cheek, trying not to laugh.

"But through it all, I've grown closer to you." He drew her hand to his lips and kissed her knuckles. "I've grown to love you."

Her eyes widened, but then she relaxed, a knowing look on her face. He slipped from his chair onto one knee, pulling out a ring box from his pants pocket. "Megan Holloway, will you marry me?"

She blinked a couple of times, as if what he'd said hadn't sunk in yet, then she gingerly took the box and opened it. She stared at the gigantic rock that ABC had purchased, a stunned look on her face. Then she plastered on a stiff smile and threw her arms around his neck. "Yes, I will marry you!" Then she elbowed him and looked at him through her eyelashes. "I thought you'd never ask."

Her reaction was totally fake. He knew it was going to be, but it still sent a small thrill through him to have her say yes to his proposal. *His pretend proposal*, he reminded himself. This wasn't real. He had to keep that in his mind, otherwise he'd lose himself in this fantasy of marrying Megan.

But he couldn't do that because Megan was not into him. She was playing a part. She'd made it perfectly clear the marriage was not going to be real.

And if he wasn't careful, he'd end up with a broken heart.

*A*s soon as Megan accepted Adam's proposal, they whisked her away and reminded her that she had signed a contract promising she wouldn't reveal the outcome of the show or she'd have to give back the hundred thousand, be responsible for other fees for damages, and give up her first born. She hid the ring, and she and Adam weren't to be seen together. Even their morning show went to reruns.

Being out of the public eye for a couple of months helped Megan relax. It was almost like she wasn't even engaged. She was flown to LA in a super-secret jet for a gown fitting, but other than that, she had nothing to do with the wedding planning. The rest of the summer flew by, and before she knew it, the show was on the air.

Megan was amazed at how, through editing and camera angles, they were able to make Adam look like he was completely smitten with her. Even she found herself rooting for Adam to win her heart. They had also managed to make Luc, Anthony, and Kyle look like real contenders. They had cut and spliced until the kisses with each guy looked heated and she appeared to be struggling to decide between them. When Kyle left the show, they made that into a huge cliffhanger episode, implying that the reason he left was because he was in love with her and didn't think he could win above Adam.

The show skyrocketed to the top of the charts, and Megan found herself in a whirlwind of activity. She was suddenly faced with the kind of popularity she'd never dreamed possible. People recognized her everywhere she went. Her email box quickly filled, and her phone rang constantly. It seemed absurd, but she decided to hire a personal assistant to handle all the requests for interviews and appearances.

The day after the proposal aired, she and Adam were flown to LA to hit the talk show circuit. Suddenly, they had to act like a happily engaged couple. Megan found herself backstage at the Ellen show, twisting her engagement ring nervously as she waited for them to usher her in front of the cameras. Adam was already talking to Ellen, but she couldn't hear what they were saying.

A guy with an earpiece and black T-shirt motioned for her to follow him. She stepped out onto the stage, the bright lights and screaming fans hitting her. She forced a smile and a polite wave. The cheers grew louder.

Adam stood and crossed the stage. He pulled her into an embrace, and whispered into her ear, "You okay?"

She nodded, even though it was a lie.

He pulled back, grinned, then kissed her. It started out normal, but soon a passion grew, a hunger in his kiss she'd never felt before. Her pulse raced, and electricity tingled through her. When he broke the kiss, she raised her eyebrow in an unspoken question, trying to catch her breath.

"I've missed you," he said in his sultry tone, much to the delight of the crowd, who went wild with hoots and cat calls. They made their way to their seats, her head still spinning from the kiss.

Ellen laughed. "You have had to keep your engagement a secret until today. How has that been for you?"

Adam slung his arm around her shoulders. "It's been torture. I've wanted to shout out to the world, 'She's mine, so get your slimy French lips off her!'" He winked, and a blush touched Megan's cheeks.

Ellen grinned at that. "He was good looking. It must have been hard watching her date and kiss other men. Especially when they all looked like that." She pointed behind them, where a photo of the guys from the show splashed on screen. They were posed, putting all the models from GQ to shame.

Adam's arm tightened around her. "Yes. But I really didn't get to watch what happened on their dates until the show aired."

Megan was surprised how pained his expression came across. Dang, he was a good actor. He actually looked upset. If he only knew what had really gone on, how disgusting Luc's slobbery kiss had been, or how juvenile Anthony was. The cameras had made him look like a smooth rock star. She bit back a giggle and tried to pay attention to what Ellen was saying.

"Now you're engaged, and the wedding is only two weeks away. How romantic, getting married in Acapulco."

Two weeks. That was all there was left before the fake wedding. She swallowed the lump in her throat. Strike that. The wedding would be real. A real minister…a real marriage certificate. She glanced down at her hand. Even a real ring. And though she didn't want to admit it, she couldn't deny her love for Adam was real as well.

She shook her head. What did she think she was doing?

~

Show after show, Megan came onstage to be greeted with a kiss by Adam. And each time, the kisses knocked her off kilter. Why did he have to do that?

Listening to the audience, she knew why. They loved it when he kissed her like he wanted to devour her for dinner. She, however, was coming undone. If he didn't stop, she was going to inject her lips with Botox to numb them up so she could keep her head on straight.

The one nice thing about her busy schedule was the fact that she had no time to fret about the wedding. When it finally arrived, she hadn't even worked herself up over it. She'd been too busy.

But now, staring at herself in the mirror while a zillion people buzzed around her yanking her hair and applying makeup, it finally sunk in. Today she would get married. To Adam.

When they finally had her hair and makeup perfect, she slipped into her dress. Some designer had made it especially for this event. It was gorgeous, of course. Form fitting until it flared out below her waist, with pearls and lace, and a material that shimmered. She felt like a beauty queen wearing it.

Someone attached a train to the back and a veil to her head, and she was ushered into a room for photos. Apparently they were afraid she wouldn't look as good after the ceremony, because they spent an excruciatingly long time capturing her image in a zillion different poses. Then she was shoved into another room for a live pre-ceremony interview.

She sat on a hard wooden chair and stared at Doctor Lemon, trying her best not to smack the smug look off her face.

"So, Megan, today is your wedding day. How do you feel about marrying Adam, after all that's happened?"

The question paired with the look on the woman's face startled Megan. What was she doing? Was this when she would confess to being a fake? When everyone would laugh at Megan for being so gullible? She gritted her teeth and took in a deep breath. "It's my wedding day. How do you think I feel?"

Doctor Lemon laughed. "You're right, wedding days are full of crazy emotions." She clasped her hands together and rested them on her knee, studying Megan. "It took you a long time to admit to having real feelings for Adam. When did you realize it?"

The past few months flashed through Megan's mind. Honestly, she'd fallen for him on that first stupid date.

Watching him eat that macaroni and cheese with his chocolate milk. And then that kiss. She'd been in trouble from the beginning. But she couldn't say that. "It became clear to me while doing the show that Adam was the one for me."

A slight frown crossed Doctor Lemon's face, but she smoothed it out. "What do you like most about Adam?"

There were too many things she liked about him. That was the problem. His deep, sexy voice. The way his dimples made the butterflies in her stomach multiply. The way he'd set her at ease for his fake proposal. His knee-weakening kisses. That masculine smell of his—she cleared her throat. Best not to think about those things. "The way he thinks of me first."

That seemed to please the faker. "Any plans for after the wedding?"

Yes. Megan planned on getting as far away from him as possible. She forced a tight smile. "We're honeymooning here in Acapulco. Then…" she shrugged. "I guess we start normal married life."

Doctor Lemon ended the interview soon after. Then they shoved her into a lobby to wait for the ceremony to begin. She knew it was an outside wedding, but that was all she'd been told. As she waited with the camera man for someone to come get her, the door opened and her father emerged.

"Daddy?" Megan's throat closed. She couldn't believe it. It had been over two years. He opened his arms, and she ran into his embrace. He wore a stylish black tuxedo, and his salt-and-pepper hair was a lot more salt than the last time she'd seen him.

"I wouldn't miss my baby girl's wedding."

His face blurred, and she blinked back the tears. "I didn't know they were bringing you here." Emotions surged through her, constricting her heart. No matter how old she got, or how accomplished she felt, being with her father turned the clock back and she became Daddy's little girl again.

"They wanted me to surprise you." His gravelly voice melted over her like butter. Even though her wedding was a sham, she still appreciated having her father to walk her down the aisle.

"And Mom?" She held her breath, surprised at how much she wanted her mother there. Their relationship had always been rocky at best.

His gaze flickered down, which said it all. "She couldn't come."

"More like she didn't approve." Megan clenched her hands into tight fists. She'd never been able to earn her mother's approval.

Her father patted her on the back. "She tries."

Megan glanced at the camera and held in a smirk. Now was not the time or place to have this conversation, so she let it go.

Her father smiled. "Wendy's here."

A surge of warmth spread through her for her sister. "I'm so glad she came."

"Wouldn't miss it for the world. Was bouncing on her seat the entire time." He grinned. "Between you and me, I think she's hoping to steal Adam away from you."

A moment later they were ushered down a hallway, through another part of the resort, and then outside. She gasped. Hundreds of white flowers lined the aisle and hung from a trellis on a small stage where Adam and the minister stood. A few rows of chairs wrapped in blue and white fabric stood on either side of the aisle, and she recognized a few faces. Wendy turned and waved at her, looking like she was about to fall out of her seat with excitement. She saw a couple of her childhood friends and a college roommate. Adam's father sat in the front row next to a couple of care takers from the facility, a beaming smile on his face. As soon as they emerged from the building, a violinist began playing the wedding march.

Her father held out his arm, and she grasped it like a life line. This was it. She really was marrying Adam. As she neared him, she could see the dimples on his face, his smile seeming genuine. His clear, blue eyes held a hint of mirth as he took her hand.

The music stopped, and the minister began the ceremony. The words floated around her, and she stared off at the crashing waves of the sea, trying not to throw up. Adam said his vows, and then it was her turn. Panic gripped her, but Adam's steady gaze helped calm her down. He squeezed her hand reassuringly, and it helped her focus. She said her lines, and after the 'I do's they exchanged rings.

And then came the kiss.

CHAPTER 22

There were a few moments in Megan's life that neared perfection. Walking across the stage to get her diploma. Her first job interview when she knew she nailed it. The phone call when she was hired at KLKX. But none of them topped her first kiss as Mrs. Adam Warner.

As soon as the minister proclaimed, "You may kiss the bride," Adam's warm arms wrapped around her, pulling her near. The smell of his musky cologne sent her heart into overdrive. His soft lips skimmed hers, teasing, sending chills over her, stirring desire from deep within. She responded without thinking, deepening the kiss, pulling him closer. He must have taken that as encouragement because his fingers entwined in her hair and suddenly the world tilted on its axis. Sparks shot through her, and Adam softly moaned. When they broke apart she wondered if the kiss was going to be allowed on national television.

The audience clapped and they were ushered off for another photo shoot. After a zillion photos of the two of them, they did all the other normal wedding things: the cake —which she successfully smeared all over Adam's face, the dinner and dancing, and the tossing of the bouquet. All the while, Megan waited for the announcement that would make her look like a fool.

Except the announcement never came.

After the guests left, the cameras turned off, and Megan and Adam went to the Bridal suite, it finally hit her. They hadn't done it. The big reveal hadn't happened.

Confused, she locked herself in the bathroom and slipped off her dress. Maybe Leon had changed his mind. A weight lifted from her shoulders.

The show was over. They'd fulfilled their contract. She and Adam were free to ride out the publicity wave and then get a quiet annulment after everyone forgot about them.

It wouldn't be too bad. Adam had already volunteered to sleep on the sofa in their honeymoon suite. And he had assured her he had a nice guest bedroom in his home. They'd just wait this out. She could do that. Right?

She stared at herself in the mirror. The frumpy sweats and T-shirt she'd brought did nothing for her figure. That was on purpose. She didn't want to give Adam the wrong idea. She brushed her teeth, then exited the bathroom.

Adam was sitting on the couch, wearing pajamas and a pair of leather slippers. She about swallowed her tongue. He patted the sofa in a silent invitation to join him.

She didn't realize how tired she was until she sat down. The thing with Doctor Lemon must have been weighing heavily on her, because she suddenly felt light and quite comfortable sitting next to Adam. "I think today went well."

He grinned. "Just well?"

"As well as it could have. I didn't trip over my dress and show everyone on national television my underwear."

Adam raised his eyebrow, and a devilish look played across his face. "Why, what kind of underwear are you wearing?"

She whacked his arm. "You'll never find out."

He laughed, but his smile didn't reach his eyes. "You looked tense today."

"I was. I really thought Doctor Lemon was going to—" She cut herself off, realizing what she was about to say.

"Was going to what?" Adam stared at her, a curious look on his face.

No way was she going to tell him she knew Doctor Lemon was a fake. "You know how she always likes to embarrass me. I wasn't sure what she'd do on our wedding day. Thank goodness all she did was one last interview."

"You should relax." He motioned for her to turn her back to him. "It's all over now."

She turned, and he began kneading her shoulders. His strong, warm hands sent little electric zings through her, which she tried to ignore. The pressure he applied to her muscles felt so good, she didn't want him to stop. "Mmm. Nice."

He kept going, working his way across her shoulders, up her neck and down her back. "You looked amazing today." His breath tickled her ear, and she realized how close he was to her.

She froze. "Um, thanks."

"Now, come on. I didn't mean it like that." He sounded annoyed at her for getting the wrong impression. "You're all tense again."

"Sorry. I thought maybe you were trying to—"

"I know what you thought." He chuckled and continued to massage her shoulders. "Not that I wouldn't like to seduce you. But I know your rules, and I intend to keep them."

She should have been happy about that statement, but for some reason she felt a little disappointed. Mentally shaking her head, she sighed. No, she did not need to be wishing for a physical relationship with Adam. That was trouble wrapped in pain. What she needed to do was hold on and wait for this to all end. "Good. Because you guys are all alike. All the physical fun with no emotional attachment."

He stopped mid-knead. "Is that what you think of me?" He turned her around, and when she wouldn't meet his gaze he hooked her chin with his finger, forcing her to look in his cool, blue eyes. "You have it all wrong."

She blinked. What did he mean? As if he read her mind, he continued. "You think I don't have an emotional attachment to you? You've got to be kidding. I've shared things with you I've never told anyone. These past few months have been…" His voice trailed off, and she found herself holding her breath, waiting for the rest of it.

His jaw clenched, and he swallowed, his Adam's apple bobbing. "Those things I said…I meant them." His voice was so quiet she almost didn't hear that last part.

What things? What was he talking about? She tried to ask, but the words stuck in her throat.

"When I told Doctor Lemon I loved you, I wasn't pretending."

Holy cow. Did he just say that? Her mouth went dry, and she stared at him. Was he for real? This had to be a joke, right? A lame attempt at spending his wedding night doing something other than sleeping on the couch. She whacked him on the arm for the second time that night. "Shut up. You dork. You almost had me." She laughed, but he didn't return her smile.

"I'm not kidding."

Really? He confessed his love to her for real, and she told him she thought he was joking? Called him a dork? What kind of an idiot was she? "Uh…" Oh, now she was really showing her brilliance. Why couldn't she think of anything intelligent to say? What does a person say after showing how amazingly craptastic they are?

He lowered his head and stared at the carpet. "I'm sorry. I should have told you. I guess I hoped you'd figure it out as we went along."

Silence stretched out between them. What was she supposed to say? That she had feelings for him too? That she hated the thought of splitting up and never seeing him again? If she told him how she was feeling, he would think she wanted to stay married.

But that's not what she wanted at all. Her career was finally taking off. She had things she wanted to do. Being married wasn't in her plan.

Adam lifted his gaze. "Do you not feel anything when we kiss?"

That's one she could answer honestly. "Of course. But that's just hormones."

"What about all the time we've spent together? Have you not felt anything for me?"

He might as well have shot her in the chest. A gaping hole opened up where her heart used to be. How was she supposed to answer him? She cleared her throat, hoping for a few more seconds to collect her thoughts. "Adam…" She put her hand on his knee. Big mistake. Tingles spread up her arm, and she removed it like he had stung her. "I like you. I just don't…"

She couldn't do it. She couldn't finish. It wasn't only the fact that she would hurt him by saying it. It wasn't true. She did love him.

"Stop." He stood and crossed the room, facing the window. "You don't have to say it. I get it."

"No, Adam, I—"

"Don't. Okay?" He ran his hand through his hair. "Just leave."

She blinked back the tears threatening to spill down her

cheeks. How had this evening gotten so messed up? She fled to the bedroom and shut the door, her hands shaking.

A part of her wanted to go back out there. To pull Adam into her arms and tell him the truth. Another part of her couldn't handle it, because she hadn't allowed herself to fully accept the truth herself. She didn't know what to do, so she crawled into bed and cried herself to sleep.

～

Adam stared out the window. Dumb, dumb, dumb. Why had he done that? Things were going so well. Megan was beginning to relax. She was starting to come around, he could tell. Why had he blurted out how he felt about her?

The minute the words were out, her invisible walls went up. She shuttered her feelings and withdrew from him. He'd scared her away.

He was an idiot.

He raked his hand through his hair again. There wasn't anything else to do. He'd spilled it all, and he couldn't take it back. Now she would run from him, and he'd be left standing with nothing but a sham of a marriage.

He crossed the room and flopped down on the couch.

There'd be no sleeping tonight.

～

Megan awoke with a start. She clutched the fabric of her T-shirt. It wasn't a dream. Adam had said he loved her, for real. That he wasn't pretending.

And she had rejected him.

Her heart hammered in her chest so loud she thought the

neighbors would hear. What had she done? Why had she refused to tell him how she felt?

There was no reason she couldn't pursue her career and stay with Adam. Why had she been so stupid?

She flopped back on her bed and stared at the ceiling. Thoughts of Adam swirled through her mind. His face when he'd found out he would have to sing in front of people. The way he had held her when she was terrified on the climbing wall. His kiss yesterday.

How could she leave him? She loved him. Megan let that sink into her head. She'd been in love with him this whole time. She'd just been pushing those feelings away.

Why? Because she'd thought he was in this to trick her. So everyone would laugh at her for believing the stupid Doctor Lemon. And then the contract with ABC had come around and she'd thought he was just doing it for the hundred thousand dollars.

A surge of emotion swelled. But he had said it was real. And the way he'd said it, he was serious. She believed him. And she loved him back.

She swallowed the golf-ball sized lump in her throat. She had to tell him. She couldn't let him think she'd been pretending this whole time.

A thrill of excitement shivered through her. She would do it. Now. She had to.

On shaking legs, she walked to the door and opened it. A blanket lay on the couch, folded neatly beside a pillow. She peeked around the corner, but the bathroom was empty.

And that was when she noticed the note.

CHAPTER 23

Megan rushed over to the table and picked up the small folded piece of paper. Her vision blurred as she read the words.

I'm sorry, Megan. I can't go through with this. I will contact a lawyer for an annulment. I'm sorry if this hurts your chances to further your career. I won't say anything to anyone. Hopefully they won't find out. —Adam

She rushed to the closet and threw open the doors. His clothes were gone. He'd left. She sunk to the floor and grabbed her head.

No.

This couldn't mean the marriage was over. Not now. Not before she had the chance to tell him. She'd been so stupid. How could she have let him go?

Her chest tightened, and she blinked away the tears. She had to make this right. She'd hurt him so terribly. Senselessly. Why had she been so selfish?

Her hands shook as she brushed the moisture from her face. She could fix this. She had to. Shaking, she stood and crossed the room to pick up her cell phone. It was cold and heavy in her hands. She dialed his number and listened to it ring. No answer.

She hung up and dialed again. Still nothing. Was he blocking her calls? Of course. He didn't want to talk to her. What did she expect? He had basically put his heart out on a line for her. And she'd smashed it.

If he wouldn't take her calls, then the only thing left to do was go home and talk to him in person.

~

The noises of the airport were making Adam's head pound. He hadn't slept at all last night. His wedding night. He drew in a deep breath and let it out slowly. This was not how he planned to spend his honeymoon.

He'd been hoping the time alone with Megan would be enough to show her how he really felt. The plan had been to ease her into the idea of them staying married. He'd really screwed that up. Handled it like a fool.

He expelled another breath. Maybe this was for the best. Megan didn't love him. Even if they'd had a wonderful honeymoon together, that wouldn't have changed her feelings for him. If she didn't have those feelings now, nothing he could do would force it upon her.

Leaving was his only choice. He knew that now. He couldn't stand to pretend to be married to her, pining after something he could never have, while she broke his heart every time she looked at him. Getting away from her was the only solution.

A woman brushed by him then stopped and turned. "You're Adam Warner." Her eyes grew wide. "I just loved your show. And your live wedding…it was so romantic." Her gaze traveled over the terminal. "Are you and Megan leaving so soon? I thought you were honeymooning here."

What was he supposed to say to that? He one-shoulder shrugged. "We decided to go somewhere else. More privacy." He winked, and the woman blushed.

"Oh, that makes perfect sense." She looked around again. "Tell Megan I hope you enjoy your honeymoon."

His stomach soured. "Of course." The woman bustled away and got lost in the crowd. He hoped that wouldn't happen again. He wasn't sure he could continue to keep this up.

They announced his flight was boarding, and he stood and dragged his carry on up to the desk. The man ahead of him must have been a heavy smoker, because the smell of tobacco and stale smoke hung thick in the air.

He had two weeks off for his honeymoon, and he didn't plan on returning home. The ticket in his hand said LA. Adam's plan was to meet with his agent and go over some of the opportunities that had come his way since the show had aired and become so popular. After finding another job, he would turn in his resignation at KLKX. He couldn't keep doing the morning show with Megan. It would be too painful.

Even though the thought of moving on was appealing, he couldn't get his heart into it. He'd miss working at the small town station. The wacky banter with Megan. The way she put him in his place. He shook his head. Getting over Megan was going to take a while. He handed his paper to the boarding agent and entered the jet way.

The thing that he didn't understand was how Megan couldn't have any feelings for him. He was sure she was attracted to him. How could she not be, when she responded to his kisses like she had?

Frustration overwhelmed him as he plopped down in his

seat. It wasn't worth rehashing again and again in his mind. She didn't want him. She'd only been acting.

He had to let it go.

~

When Megan finally stepped off the airplane at the Omaha airport, it was late and she was exhausted. A few people turned their heads and whispered behind their hands, but no one approached her. She wondered what they thought, her being alone the day after her wedding aired.

She picked up her luggage and headed for the car rental counter. She'd been carted around so much lately, it was going to be different driving herself around. Her car was parked at her apartment. Seemed like a lifetime since she'd been behind her grandmother's old Accord. Even though she could afford a new car now, something told her she wouldn't be trading it in anytime soon.

By the time she arrived home, it was too late to go see Adam. She let herself in her apartment and dragged in her suitcases. She'd go see him first thing in the morning.

Sleep evaded her, and she ended up tossing and turning all night. Why hadn't she just taken the time to process her feelings earlier? Why had she reacted the way she had when he told her he loved her? She rolled over again. She had to talk to him.

When sunlight finally came through her window, she was ready. A quick shower and some make up, and she was out the door.

It didn't take long to drive to Adam's house. The porch still sagged, and paint was still peeling off the sides of the house. No dog bounded up to meet her this time. The house stood still, no sign of life. Was he not back yet?

She climbed the steps and looked in the window. She couldn't see much. She knocked on the door. No response. Where was Adam? She waited for another minute before pounding again. "Adam, open the door!"

"He's not here."

The small voice behind her startled her and she jumped, turning around. A young boy stood in the driveway, one strap of his coveralls sliding down his arm. "He's gone."

Megan put her hand to her chest. "You scared me. Where did you come from?"

The boy pointed. "I live over there."

"Ah, I see. Where did Adam go?"

The boy shrugged. "My mom said he's on a moneynoon and won't be back for a while."

The mispronunciation made her smile. "I see."

"But don't worry, moneynoon's don't hurt. I asked." The little boy beamed up at her.

She wasn't so sure that was true. "Thanks."

Megan left Adam's house, frustrated and broken. She tried his cell again, with no luck. She refused to leave him a message. There was no way she was going to tell him she loved him in a voice mail, let alone a text. She needed a different plan.

And then it hit her. She still had some shows with Adam scheduled in. After the wedding appearances. Adam couldn't skip them. They were in the contract.

If she could get Leon to work something out, she could come clean in a way that Adam couldn't ignore. She picked up her phone. The seconds ticked by as she waited for Leon to answer his line, her heart pounding. If he would go for this, he might get the biggest publicity stunt yet. He answered with a quick hello.

"Leon, it's Megan. Listen, something happened."

"What?"

She chewed her bottom lip. "Um, Adam left. Said he was done."

"Whoa, we've still got a few more shows lined up for you two. He can't quit now." The panic in his voice was evident.

"I know. But I have an idea."

"Wait." Leon paused, apparently thinking of what he could do to salvage the situation. "What if you guys stage a fight? Something explosive. On air! That would—"

"Leon!" She took a deep breath. "I don't want to stage a fight. I want to come clean."

A noise sounded like Leon had dropped the phone. After a moment, he came back on. "Megan, you can't do that. You've signed contracts. You know how much trouble you would be in if you did that?"

"I read my contracts. I signed one saying I wouldn't reveal the outcome of the show. Another keeping me from talking about the show before it aired. Another agreeing to marry Adam, and another agreeing to a certain number of appearances. Not one of them said I can't reveal how I truly feel about him."

"How's that going to help you? If you go on national television and tell everyone you hate Adam, your fans will turn against you. You'll ruin the show and your reputation."

She rubbed her temple, pushing herself to go on. "I don't hate Adam. That's not what I'm going to say." She steeled her nerves and plunged ahead. "I actually fell in love with him."

Another loud clunk came through the line and she was sure he'd dropped the phone again. "What? You did?"

"I know it sounds stupid, and I can't explain it, but as Adam and I pretended to have a relationship, I found myself falling for him. I'm in love with him." When Leon didn't say anything, she added, "For real."

Leon softly swore under his breath. "Are you serious?"

She ignored his question. "The thing is, Adam told me basically the same thing. He fell in love with me as well."

"Wait, what? Why did he leave you then?"

Heat flooded her face as she remembered her wedding night. "His admission shocked me. I wasn't ready yet to admit how I felt. So I sort of told him I didn't feel the same."

"Oh, that's cold, woman."

"I know. I wasn't thinking straight. But now I have to tell him, you see?" She stared at the suitcase beside her bed, still unpacked. "I have to tell him the truth."

She could feel Leon's excitement building on the other end of the phone. "You've got to be kidding me. Are you serious?"

"We're scheduled to appear on the Penelope Jones show next week. I want to come clean. With *all* of it."

Silence. She knew that would make him squirm. "What do you mean, all of it?"

"I know about Doctor Lemon. I know the first show was a setup, the machine was fake, the whole bit. If I'm going to do this, I'm going to tell all of it."

Leon sucked in his breath and didn't say anything for a minute, probably letting it sink in. "When did you find out?"

That wasn't the question she had expected. "I overheard you and Adam talking after our first date."

Leon laughed, which surprised her. "Ah, the karaoke makes so much more sense now."

"Yeah, ha ha, funny. I was really hurt, Leon. You'd planned to humiliate me on television." As she spoke, the old pain bubbled up again.

"Hey, it wasn't personal."

"What if I drag you into this, on the Penelope Jones show? Make America hate you for what you did. Would it be personal then?"

He sucked in a breath like he were going to argue with

her, but then stopped. It was as if she could see the wheels turning in his head. She imagined his face, maybe draining of color, as it sunk in. "You're right. I wouldn't like that." Another moment of silence came. "I'm sorry, Megan."

"You're a good guy, Leon. Just a little too ambitious. Try to take it down a notch, okay? Or someday, someone is going to turn the tables on you."

"You're all right, Megan." He sounded submissive. Maybe he knew what she could do to his name if she dragged him into this.

A smile crept across her face. "I knew you'd understand. Now, here's what I want you to do for the Penelope Jones show."

CHAPTER 24

Megan wasn't surprised when Leon called to tell her Adam had turned in his resignation to the station. She knew she'd hurt him. And now she knew he wasn't coming back. Her plan had to work, or she'd lose everything.

The Penelope Jones show was in two days, and Leon was working on getting everything ready. If she could go through with this, she might be able to get Adam back.

~

Adam paced the green room of the Penelope Jones show, his stomach tied in knots. The past few days had been torture. He couldn't sleep at night. He couldn't eat. All he could do was kick himself for messing things up with Megan. And now he was here, ready to go out on the set where she sat. He had to pretend everything was fine.

How could he do that? He wasn't that good of an actor.

His signal came that it was time to go on the show, and he obediently stepped out on stage. His first glimpse of Megan stopped his heart. Her blonde hair was pulled up off her shoulders, and she wore a dress that showed off all her curves. He swallowed and smiled at the audience. They screamed in response.

Penelope gave him a hug and sat down. His chair was beside Megan, but not so close that he had to put his arm around her or hold her hand, and he blew out a breath of relief. He made himself comfortable in the chair and stared out at the audience. Maybe if he ignored Megan, he could get through this without too much heartache.

"Megan and I were just talking about your morning show." Penelope grinned at him, a sort of hungry look on her face that he couldn't quite understand.

He raised his eyebrows. "Yes?"

"She was just explaining how she hated you." The smile widened.

Megan shook her head. "No, I think hate is a strong word. But we did butt heads. Do we have a clip or two?"

The crowd cheered as the screen started up. Their morning show appeared, he and Megan bantering. He said something about her hair, and her lips tightened. Then she came back with one of her classic zingers. The audience laughed. The next clip went about the same way, with him implying she was less of a woman because she was single, and her quick witted response, putting him in his place.

He saw the way she stiffened when he said those things. The way her smile froze, her eyes narrowed, and it struck him. Penelope was right. She hated him.

How could he have said those things to her? How could he have not seen how it affected her? He had been so mean. No wonder she couldn't return his feelings. He'd been horrible to her.

The audience grew silent after the clips ended. Megan

turned to Penelope. "As you can see, Adam and I weren't exactly best friends."

Penelope leaned forward. "But wasn't that just sexual tension?"

Megan shook her head. "Definitely not. I honestly didn't like the guy."

Adam forgot his resolve to not look at her and stared. What was she doing?

"I think it's time to bring out our third guest."

Third guest? It wasn't until then that he noticed the other empty chair beside him. Adam jerked his gaze over to the stage entrance.

Doctor Lemon stepped out, crossed the stage, and sat down. Confusion clouded his brain. What was going on? This was supposed to be a routine appearance. The doctor wasn't on the schedule.

Megan cleared her throat. "If I'm going to come clean, I can't ignore our good friend, Doctor Shelby Lemon."

Come clean? A sinking feeling started in his chest and moved to his stomach. What was Megan doing?

She continued to speak. "You see, the day we had Doctor Lemon on our show, I was shocked to find out Adam had some kind of buried feelings for me. If I'm going to be totally honest, I must admit that even though I didn't like the guy, I found him physically attractive."

Where was she going with this? He tried not to squirm.

"And when the machine said he had hidden, deeper feelings for me, I was kind of blindsided. I mean, ladies, who doesn't like to find out an attractive man likes them?" The women in the audience all cheered.

"When did you find out the truth?" Penelope's face grew serious.

The truth? Oh, no. She wasn't going to…Megan didn't know. Right? He swallowed.

"After Adam and I had our first date, I found out the website was telling people to stay tuned for our second date. I was furious. That's when I went down to the station and overheard Adam talking to our producer."

Everyone in the room froze, and Adam couldn't breathe. She'd known this whole time.

"What did you overhear?"

Megan turned and pointed to Doctor Lemon. "That she is a *fake*."

The audience gasped, and the doctor's face blanched.

Megan continued. "She's not a real doctor. The machine was a setup. She was controlling it the whole time."

Doctor Lemon jumped up, her composure lost. "This is an outrage!" Unfortunately, the force of her movement dislodged her wig, making it sit on her head askew.

The audience laughed until Doctor Lemon stormed off the stage. All Adam could do was stare in disbelief. It was then that he noticed the caption showing on the screen. "Megan Holloway Tells All." His mouth went dry.

Penelope looked like she'd won the lottery. "What did you do, when you found out Doctor Lemon wasn't real?"

Megan avoided his gaze. "I did the only thing I could think of. I got revenge."

A clip of Adam's face reading the karaoke sign flashed up on screen, and everyone went wild. He slid down a little in his seat. Why was she doing this? What had he done that was so terrible now? He'd told her he loved her. Did that offend her so much that she had to retaliate with this 'tell all' show?

Penelope turned to him for the first time. "Adam, did you know Megan had found out about Doctor Lemon?"

He blinked. She really expected him to participate in his own public hanging? Everyone waited for his response. He shook his head, because no words would come.

Penelope turned back to Megan. "How did you feel, knowing that you were being deceived?"

"I was upset, of course. But, despite everything, I was also aware that our dates were making our show more popular." She stopped, looked down at her feet, and swallowed. "I'm ashamed to admit it, but I continued to date Adam because I thought it would further my career."

The audience murmured, and Penelope held up her hand. "Before you pass judgment, let's hear the whole story. Megan, what happened next?"

"We went out a few more times. Then he hit that deer in the road."

Penelope looked up at the screen, and a clip from that night played. Adam watched himself on the screen having an emotional breakdown, holding that dying fawn by the side of the road. What was the purpose of bringing that up?

Megan blinked, and he thought for a second she was trying not to tear up, but when she spoke her voice was steady. "My opinion of him changed that night."

"How so?"

"I saw a side of him I hadn't seen. A tender side."

Adam squinted at her. What was she doing? Why did he feel like he was on a roller coaster, with no way of knowing where he would end up?

Penelope smiled at the camera. "I think we all got to see that." She turned back to Megan. "Then the next thing I remember seeing was you losing it."

Another clip rolled, this one of Megan shouting about not ever marrying Adam, even if she were dying and he was the only cure. The audience laughed, and Megan blushed. "Not my best moment."

"Why were you so angry?"

"Leon was trying to manipulate the show. He was online encouraging our fans to push for marriage." Megan took a breath, still avoiding his gaze. "I didn't like being coerced. I felt played. I got angry."

"But then why would you agree to be on the ABC show, Winning Megan Over?"

Another blush touched her cheeks. "I was told it would be a dating show, and to be totally honest, I did it to further my career again."

The audience frowned and whispered amongst themselves. But Megan didn't stop there. "They were also offering us a hundred thousand dollars to do the show."

Adam silently groaned. This was definitely a 'tell all' show. Megan wasn't going to stop until she'd given every gory detail. Why she was doing this was clear. She was releasing him from any more contact with her. She was doing this so they could go their separate ways.

Without coming out like this, they would have to make up excuses as to why they weren't living together. They'd have to lie, and say they'd had a fight, were separated, or some other such thing. They'd have to lie until they got a divorce. She was doing this to give him an out.

But he didn't want her to take all the blame. He was part of this too. "I talked her into it," he blurted.

They both stared at him. When Penelope had gotten over her shock, she quietly urged, "Go on."

"I wanted the money. ABC was only willing to do the show if we agreed to get married at the end." Everyone gasped at this revelation, but he ignored them. "I convinced Megan to go ahead with it, to get married, but only on paper. She reluctantly agreed. The marriage was never supposed to be real."

The audience burst into loud chatter, and Penelope had to calm them down. "I'm being told we need to go to commercial break. We'll be right back with Megan Holloway and Adam Warner, as we learn the whole truth about their show."

As soon as the cameras were off, Megan turned to him, her eyes accusing. "What are you doing?"

"I could ask you the same thing."

Her gaze softened. "Sorry. You just startled me. I thought you'd just sit and listen."

"Oh, believe me, I'm quite entertained by all of this. But I couldn't let you take all the blame for what happened."

She placed her hand on his knee, the gesture about driving him out of his skin. "Thank you. But this is my tell all. I need you to sit and quietly listen to the rest."

He no longer wanted to listen. All he wanted to do was to pick her up, throw her over his shoulder, and take her home so he could kiss her until she fell in love with him. Instead of admitting his caveman-like urge, he simply nodded.

"Thank you," she repeated. Then she settled back in her chair, and they waited until the break was over.

Penelope snapped back into action as soon as the cameras were rolling. "We are back with Megan Holloway and Adam Warner. Megan and Adam have just revealed that their marriage was never supposed to be real. Please tell us more about this, Megan."

Megan clutched the sides of her chair, her knuckles white. "The actual marriage is real. We used a real minister, signed real papers, and it's legally binding. Adam and I are married." She stared at the cameras. "But we agreed to it under false pretenses. We never intended to act like a real married couple."

"So, nothing went on in the bedroom, then?" Penelope gave the camera a wicked grin.

Megan shook her head. "We agreed to get married because of the show, and for the money. That's the only reason."

The audience obviously didn't like this statement, but hushed to hear what else Megan was going to say. "I knew ahead of time that I was not to fall for any of the other men on the show. They were there to create tension, but never as serious contenders. I knew Adam would propose, and I knew I was to accept."

Penelope nodded. "I think there's more to tell. Am I right?"

Megan nodded, her lips pinched tight. "What I didn't know was that Adam Warner was going to fall in love with me."

CHAPTER 25

Megan peeked over at Adam and got to see the color drain from his face. She had to keep going or she would never be able to finish. "It was our wedding night. I was to sleep in the bedroom, and Adam had agreed to be on the couch. I was tense from the stress of the fake wedding, so Adam offered to massage my shoulders."

A few ladies in the audience made noises of approval. Who wouldn't? Adam was all hunk. She was sure they were imagining him giving them a massage. She pushed away a smile. "We talked for a few minutes, but as our conversation turned more intimate, I grew uncomfortable."

Adam looked like he wanted to crawl under his chair. She hated embarrassing him like this, but she had to get everyone to understand.

Penelope rubbed her hands together. "Then what happened?"

Adam leaned forward, resting his elbows on his knees, his head in his hands. She was hurting him. She had to get the rest out. "Adam admitted to me that he had really fallen in love with me."

The audience froze, and the silence was deafening. Megan clenched her hands and tried to muster up her courage. "I freaked out. I'm ashamed to admit it, but I couldn't handle his admission at that time. I clammed up. And when he asked me if I felt anything for him, I couldn't admit my true feelings."

Adam's head snapped up, his blue eyes meeting hers in a piercing stare.

"Are you saying that you have feelings for Adam as well?"

It felt like everyone in the room was holding their breath, waiting for Megan to speak. "I do."

The room exploded in noise, and Penelope once again had to quiet everyone. "Are you in love with him?"

Megan stared at Adam, his body tense waiting for her answer, like a panther watching his prey. "Yes."

He jumped from his chair and snatched her up in a crushing hug. Before she knew it, his lips were on hers, with an intensity she'd never felt from him before. When she pulled back, he said, "You'd better not be playing me, Megan Holloway."

She threw her head back and laughed. "I'm not. I tried to tell you, but you'd left and wouldn't answer my calls."

Adam picked her up and swung her around, planting another passionate kiss on her. "You sure know how to make a guy sweat."

Penelope laughed along with the rest of the room. "If you two love birds could sit again, I do have a few more questions."

Megan pried herself away from Adam and sat. Adam took her hand in the warmth of his own. A montage of videos of them kissing displayed on the screen. Penelope motioned to the television. "America watched your passionate kisses. How did it feel, kissing Adam like this but not realizing that he was actually falling in love with you?"

"I was confused. My heart was falling for him, but in my head I knew we were supposed to be acting for the camera. Except his kisses were intoxicating."

Adam grinned at that, and wiggled his eyebrows.

"When did you finally admit to yourself that you were in love with him?"

Megan pursed her lips in thought. "I didn't allow myself to realize it until Kyle came right out and asked me. Then it hit me. I knew I had fallen for him."

Penelope's eyebrows drew together. "I don't remember Kyle asking you about Adam."

"They cut that part. Probably because it made it obvious who I would choose."

"That makes sense. Now, I only have one more question." Penelope looked between the two of them. "What are you going to do now?"

Adam spoke before she had the chance. "We're going to go on a proper honeymoon!"

The audience laughed, and Penelope shook her head, though she was smiling. "Now, Adam, loving someone and marrying them are two separate things. Are you sure Megan wants to make that kind of commitment right now?"

He turned to her, his eyes pleading. He slipped from his chair and got on one knee. The audience cheered, then quieted down so they could hear. Megan's heart jumped into her throat.

"I know we're already married, but you deserve a proper proposal." He took both of her hands. "Megan Holloway, I fell in love with you so completely, I can't imagine my life without you. Even though you enjoy putting me through torture…" He paused, glancing around at the studio and getting a chuckle from the audience. "My life would never be the same without you."

She blinked back the tears threatening to spill down her

cheeks. Adam smiled, and continued. "I would be honored to call you my wife. My real wife. Will you marry me for real?"

A few shouts of approval echoed through the room before everyone held their breath, waiting for Megan to answer. She squeezed his hands, butterflies tickling her stomach. "Yes."

The crowd went nuts. Adam pulled her up for another embrace. "You don't know how happy you've made me," he whispered in her ear.

And then the audience melted away as he gave her another toe-curling kiss.

EPILOGUE

Megan sat on the porch swing, her legs tucked under her, Adam's strong arms wrapped around her. She nestled into his chest. The sound of the evening crickets and the gentle rocking of the swing provided the perfect setting. She sighed.

"What?" Adam ran his fingers over her arm, sending tingles through her.

"Nothing. I'm just happy." She peeked up at him. "I never thought I'd have this, you know?"

The corner of his mouth lifted in a half-smile. "A porch swing?"

She giggled. "Any of it. I thought I knew what I wanted. But sitting here, with you, I can't imagine my life any other way."

"I'm glad Leon hired me back."

"He had no choice. The website blew up."

Adam kissed the top of her head. "Do you regret turning down the national show?"

She snuggled closer to him. "No. I thought fame would make me happy. It didn't."

He chuckled. "Me neither. I like it here in the country, saggy porch and all." They were quiet for a moment before he spoke again. "So, what's this surprise we're waiting for?"

"I can't tell you. Otherwise, it wouldn't be a surprise, would it?"

They watched the dusk settle in, and just as the air was getting a bit too chilly, the neighbor boy, Eli, came through the trees. A small puppy wriggled in his arms.

Megan jumped up and rushed to him. "This the one?"

"Yep. Momma said we can't keep any of this litter. Gotta find 'um good homes." The puppy snuggled into his armpit as he grinned. "I picked this one out special for you."

Adam stood. "What's this?"

Megan picked up the soft bundle. "Thanks, Eli." She ruffled his hair and sent him back home. When she turned to Adam, she couldn't decipher his expression. "I thought we could help out the neighbor kid. Maybe take in one of the pups."

The small golden retriever sniffed her shoulder, then gave it a little lick. Adam descended the steps and lifted the puppy from her arms. "He's perfect." The dog licked his face, and he laughed.

Megan's heart warmed. "I'm so glad. I was afraid with what had happened in the past…" She let her voice trail off.

"It's a time for new beginnings." He tucked the pup in the crook of his arm and took her hand. "For all of us."

The End

AFTERWORD

Thank you for reading! If you like Victorine's books, check out her bundles she has on sale on her website. You can save big with a bundle! Use the code 20OFF and get 20% off your entire order!

www.victorinelieske.com

If you want to read what Victorine is writing as she writes it, check out her Patreon. For just a few bucks a month you can get early access to her stories!: https://www.patreon.com/Victorine

Join Victorine's Newsletter and get a free novella: Her Sister's Fiancé. https://BookHip.com/CXNTMH

VICTORINE'S T-SHIRT SHOP

Sometimes the characters in Victorine's novels wear funny t-shirts. If you like them, you can buy them at Victorine's T-shirt shop.

And it's not just T-shirts, Victorine has cloth masks, mugs, and other merchandise. They're fun! Take a peek!

https://victorinelieske.threadless.com/

ABOUT THE AUTHOR

Victorine and her husband live in Nebraska with their four children and two cats. She loves all things romance, and is currently addicted to Korean Dramas, which are super swoony and romantic. (She highly recommends Crash Landing on You on Netflix.)
When she's not writing, she's designing book covers for authors or making something with her extensive yarn collection.

Made in United States
Cleveland, OH
25 May 2025